Mu
S
fing

Tamsyn Murray was born in Cornwall in the Chinese [year] of the Rat. This makes her charming, creative and [good on a good day) but also selfish, restless and [bad on a bad day).

[Having moved ar]ound a lot during her early years, she now liv[es ....] with her husband and her daughter. At least [her body] does. Her mind tends to prefer imaginary places [and it] wanders off whenever it can but that's not necessaril[y] a bad thing in a writer.

When she isn't making things up, you might find Tamsyn on the stage, pretending to be someone else. She occasionally auditions for TV talent shows. One day she might get past the first round . . .

Find out more about Tamsyn at her website:
www.tamsynmurray.co.uk

My So-Called Haunting

TAMSYN MURRAY

PICCADILLY PRESS · LONDON

First published in Great Britain in 2010
by Piccadilly Press Ltd,
5 Castle Road, London NW1 8PR
www.piccadillypress.co.uk

A catalogue record for this book is available
from the British Library

ISBN: 978 1 84812 092 1 (paperback)

3 5 7 9 10 8 6 4 2

Printed in the UK by CPI Bookmarque, Croydon, CR0 4TD
Cover design by Patrick Knowles

Mixed Sources
Product group from well-managed
forests and other controlled sources
www.fsc.org   Cert no. TT-COC-002227
© 1996 Forest Stewardship Council
FSC

For Lisa, Cathy and Alison,
who made growing up so much fun.

Chapter 1

I knew the woman on the bridge was going to jump a split second before she did.

'Wait!'

The word was out of my mouth before my brain kicked in and my fingers stretched towards the window of the bus as though dragged on invisible strings. Conversations around me stopped mid-sentence and curious stares shot my way, but I couldn't wrench my gaze away from the woman on the parapet, and everything else faded into the background. Casting one sorrowful glance over her shoulder, she launched herself into the air and plummeted to the roaring traffic below. I waited for a scream to shatter the chill morning air. It didn't come. My ears strained for the squeal of brakes and the grim crunch of metal on bone, but there was only silence.

Somehow, that was worse. My eyes closed and I swallowed a wave of sick horror. I'd just watched a woman leap to her death. The fact that I couldn't have stopped her didn't make me feel any better.

Gradually, the sounds of London's rush hour filtered through to my numbed brain. I opened my eyes to see that the traffic was on the move. The engine of the bus roared and we lurched forwards along Hornsey Lane Bridge. Around me, passengers steadied themselves and resumed their activities as though nothing unusual had happened. My outburst had been dismissed. Dotted among the random mixture of age, nationality and dress-sense were several kids in the same Heath Park C of E Secondary uniform that I wore, but it was only my second week at the school so I didn't recognise any faces.

As I gathered my jangling nerves and peered around the packed bus, one thing was obvious; not a single person had seen the woman jump. I ran a shaky hand over my face and sighed, wondering why I was surprised. They were normal people, going about their everyday lives. None of them were like me. None of them saw ghosts.

It's not as interesting as it sounds, being born into a family of psychics. OK, so your mum is much more likely to believe that there's something lurking in the cupboard at the bottom of your bed, but she'll probably encourage you to have a chat rather than chase it away. Since my mum was the only non-psychic in her family, I didn't even have that luxury. She accepted that ghosts existed, of course; it'd be hard not to when her sister and parents talked about them non-stop, but she couldn't see or hear them, and I don't think she ever really understood what it was like to see things other people didn't. I suppose that's why she became a biologist, because science dealt only with hard evidence and facts.

My dad died before I was even born. Mum didn't talk about him much, but I got the idea he hadn't been psychic. It was my aunt that I turned to when I was trying to make sense of my strange gift as I grew up, in spite of the fact that she lived in London and we were in Scotland. Blond-haired and blue-eyed like me, Celestine looked more like my older sister than my aunt, and the gift we shared meant we were on the same wavelength most of the time. When Mum was agonising over a once-in-a-lifetime opportunity to spend a year studying sea horses in the Great Barrier Reef, it was a no-brainer for me to stay with Celestine while she was away. Since GCSEs began in Year Ten, we'd decided I'd stay until I'd done my exams. Sure, I'd miss my life in Edinburgh, but I'd always been a bit of a loner, and there was always MSN for the few friends I'd had. At least I wasn't leaving a best friend behind, and as for boys – ha! Maybe a fresh start at a new school was just what I needed, and this time I planned to spend less time worrying about the dead and more time on my social life. Seriously, how hard could it be?

'Hey, Skye,' Celestine greeted me as I slouched into the kitchen after school and dropped my bag on to the floor. 'Bad day?'

I slid on to a seat at the breakfast bar and scowled first at her and then at her boyfriend, Jeremy. 'Is it that obvious?'

She finished drying the cup she was holding and dropped the tea towel next to the sink. 'Yep. Your mood is greyer than your skirt.'

I stared at her. She'd been able to second-guess my emotions for as long as I could remember. 'How do you do that? Am I the only person you read more easily than last week's *Heat*?'

Jeremy rinsed his hands under the tap. 'No, she does it to me too. You get used to it after a while.'

Celestine smiled. 'I can see your aura – it's like a glow around you, reflecting your emotions. Everyone has one, and yours is telling me you're Grumpy McGrump.'

I had read about auras before but hadn't realised my aunt could see them; no wonder her people skills were so good. She was spot on about my mood too. After the horror of the journey to school, I'd been followed off the bus by three kids who'd taken it in turns to shout out,

'Wait!' in the worst impersonations of my Scottish accent I'd ever heard. I'd scurried inside the school gates with scant minutes to spare and found that Megan, the only girl in my registration group I'd broken the ice with, was off sick. With the horrible image of the suicide ghost on replay in my brain, I'd had the attention span of a toddler on Jelly Tots in my lessons and finished the morning with a stern ticking-off from Mr Evans for daydreaming. By the time he'd let me go, there was nothing left in the canteen except for curled-up sandwiches and an overcooked sausage roll. Then, to round off the perfect Monday, I had an essay on the human reproductive system to write. Was it any wonder I wasn't doing a happy dance?

'Why can't I see auras?' I asked Celestine, trying to ignore the intense, slightly cross-eyed stare Jeremy was aiming just above my head.

'Not every psychic can. They're a bit like the faint blue glow you see around ghosts, but they're much stronger in the living and more colourful.' Celestine tilted her head and Jeremy gave up trying to see my aura. 'Why don't you tell us what's bugging you?'

I didn't need a second invitation. When I'd finished, both she and Jeremy were solemn.

'I'm not surprised you're feeling grey,' Celestine said. 'What a terrible thing to witness.'

My head slumped on to my folded arms. 'What I

don't understand is why she would jump again when she's already dead. Why put herself through that?'

'Well, assuming that's how she died, she'll be tied there and probably hasn't worked out how to leave. The rest is just force of habit, I suppose,' Celestine said, her voice filled with sadness. 'Think about it – we're supposed to go straight to the astral plane when we die, but if there's something holding us here then we don't. Some ghosts can't cope when they don't pass across, and suicides tend to find it the hardest.'

'What happened when she – you know – hit the ground?' Jeremy asked, interrupting my train of thought.

'I didn't see,' I answered, frowning slightly. 'I suppose she just sort of disappeared, but maybe she came back to the bridge and did it all again. What if she's a serial suicide?'

Oh God, I really hoped she wasn't. Settling into a new school was hard enough without seeing someone throw themselves off the bridge every time I crossed it.

Jeremy shuddered. 'Imagine what it must be like to take your own life and wake up as a ghost – you're expecting your problems to end and instead things get a thousand times worse.'

An odd tone had crept into his voice, filling me with shame at my selfish thought. It was almost as though he was speaking from experience. I knew he was part psychic, and had got to know a ghost once, but I thought she'd been a murder victim, not a suicide. Maybe there'd been other ghosts he didn't talk about.

Celestine squeezed his arm, nodding. 'Sometimes it's easier to repeat the same actions day after day than try to work out what to do next. I've seen it at the Dearly D from time to time.'

Part of her job as a psychic at the Church of the Dearly Departed, a spiritualist church in Kensal Green, involved trying to help ghosts contact their loved ones and find their way to the astral plane. I'd been with her a few times and I knew the atmosphere there was often emotionally charged. What I'd seen that morning might all be part of a day's work for her, but I knew she cared about each and every spirit she met and felt duty-bound to do whatever she could for them. It was something else we had in common, which I guess is why the woman on the bridge had affected me so much.

'She seemed so young. I wonder who she was,' I said, remembering the desperation etched on to her face.

'We'll probably never know,' Jeremy replied, his tone subdued. 'It's a popular place for suicide.'

Perfect, just what I needed; my route to school passed through a haunting hotspot. Who knew what I'd see tomorrow?

'I could give you a lift sometimes, if you like?' Jeremy said, clearly picking up on my worried expression. 'Save you getting the bus every day.'

I threw him a grateful smile. He might have the fashion sense of Mr Bean but he was all right, really. 'That'd be great, thanks.'

I'd just have to pray no one saw me getting out of his deeply uncool Nissan Micra. In fact, maybe it'd be better if he dropped me off round the corner. I chewed my lip doubtfully. Actually, it would probably be safest to walk.

My stomach rumbled mid-thought, reminding me of my unsatisfactory lunch. A missed meal might help my waistline, but I'd never been one for diets.

'OK,' I said, jumping down from my seat and heading towards the fridge. 'Is there any of that banoffee pie left? Maybe a slice would help with my bad mood.'

Celestine raised a questioning eyebrow. 'Oh, your aura is fine now. Besides, you wouldn't want to spoil your dinner, would you?'

'And there's only one piece left and it's got my name on it,' Jeremy put in. 'So don't get any ideas.'

I stared wistfully at the wedge of cream-covered pie for a full five seconds before heaving a melodramatic sigh and closing the fridge.

'I suppose I'll make do with an apple for now then,' I said, reaching a grudging hand towards the fruit bowl. 'But I'm not sure you're going to want that pie, Jeremy. I saw Mary licking it earlier.'

Celestine and Jeremy didn't live alone. Their house

was in a leafy street in a posh bit of Highgate and it had been built on land that once upon a time had been a farm. We had the dubious pleasure of being haunted by Mary Drover, a sixteenth century witch with an attitude that was over four hundred years out of date. Since I'd moved in two weeks ago, we'd grown an instant hate-hate relationship and she never missed a chance to stir up trouble for me. Naturally, I returned the favour whenever I could.

My aunt wasn't buying it this time, though. She looked at me closely and grinned. 'No, she didn't.'

Oh great, so now she could tell from my aura if I was fibbing? Sighing, I snatched up my bag and went up to my room, making a mental note to save any little white lies for text messages in future. Like I said, sometimes having a psychic family sucked.

Chapter 2

There's a lot of rubbish out there about ghosts. Like the idea that being dead somehow turns you into some kind of psycho – if I had a pound for every time I've heard a story about an evil spirit luring unsuspecting tourists over a cliff, I'd be sorted for mascara money for the next few years. The truth is that ghosts generally have their own problems and don't have the time or the inclination to go around bumping off the living. There were one or two exceptions, but weren't there always? It didn't mean *Paranormal Activity* was a fly-on-the-wall documentary.

That said, for some reason Mary Drover was determined to be my own personal banshee. I'd tried being nice to her but she still took massive delight in tormenting me. She'd also developed a seriously inappropriate habit of walking into my bedroom unannounced. Like if she decided it was time I was up on a Saturday morning when my body had other plans. Or when I was trying to decide whether shortening my skirt would help me win friends at Heath Park. I'd never got to the bottom of why she hadn't passed across centuries ago, but she was a major pain in the arse to me.

'How many times do I have to ask you to knock?' I yelled at her as she drifted through the door of my room on Tuesday morning and looked me up and down. Like most ghosts, she floated a couple of centimetres above the floor, as though she was sticking up two metaphorical fingers at us mere mortals bound by the laws of gravity.

'Thou resemblest a strumpet,' she said, staring pointedly at my thigh-skimming skirt. Sometimes I had trouble understanding Mary's weird cross-century babbling but in this case I was getting her loud and clear. She didn't approve of my uniform adjustments and was threatening to grass me up.

'Everyone wears them like this now,' I announced, eyeing my reflection in the mirror and wondering if the extra inches of leg on view would earn me the nickname Thunder Thighs. 'If you had your way, I'd go to school wearing a smock.'

She sniffed. 'It would be more seemly.'

Never at my best early in the morning, my patience evaporated. 'I don't have time for this, Mary. What do you want?'

'Thy aunt made mention of a spirit who throws herself from the bridge of the horseless carriages.'

I stared at her, wondering why she was so interested. 'That's right.'

She raised a finger. 'Thou should not meddle with unwilling spirits. Not all are ready to pass across.'

I couldn't help wondering whether she was speaking from personal experience. Maybe someone had tried to get rid of her in the past – I could certainly sympathise if they had. Squeezing past, I yanked open my bedroom door. 'Just because you're not ready to move on doesn't mean no one else is.'

Scowling, she followed me along the landing. 'Heed my words, leave well alone!'

I went into the bathroom and reached for my toothbrush. It wasn't there. 'Whoever this woman is, she threw herself off a bridge. How exactly am I going to make things worse for her? And where is my toothbrush?'

She leaned in closer. 'There are those who would seek to hurt even the most tormented soul. Thy well-meant efforts may drive this spirit to further harm.'

I sighed. Could she be any more cryptic? 'I've got no idea what you're on about. Have you seen my toothbrush?'

She raised her chin defiantly. 'Promise me thou wilt desist in thy efforts and I will reveal the location of thy mouth-scourge.'

I counted to ten under my breath and, not for the first

time, wondered about exorcism. 'I will not,' I said firmly. 'But if it's any consolation, you've made me late so I probably won't see her today anyway. Now give me the toothbrush.'

Her gaze slid towards the toilet bowl. 'It is behind the privy.'

Urgh. I wouldn't be putting that in my mouth again any time soon, then.

'Fine. I needed a new one anyway.' Stepping back, I closed the bathroom door in her face. 'And don't even think about coming in here or I know one spirit I'll be seriously meddling with. Haven't you ever heard of privacy?'

I half expected Mary to follow me to school. I mean, technically it was possible for her to do it; ghosts weren't completely tied to their haunting zone – the place where they'd died – as long as they carried an original item from that place with them. Mary favoured an antique silver letter-opener, honed to a wicked point through decades of use, and was prone to brandishing it like Lord Voldemort whenever she lost her temper. I'd never got close enough to find out if she could actually cut me with it and could only hope she never encountered a psychic mugger. Even with the letter-opener tucked under her ragged clothes, she couldn't stay away from home indefinitely. Since I knew for a fact that her

Monday nights were spent with a ghostly witches' coven in Finchley, I also knew she'd have to spend some time at home the next day to recharge – ghosts could leave their haunting zone for up to a day at a time, but they needed to return at regular intervals. Whatever the reason, there was no sign of Mary as I walked along Hornsey Lane.

Predictably, I was late and there was no sign of any ghosts on the busy bridge. Yet again I found myself hurrying through the school gates, hoping I'd make it to registration before I landed myself in detention, but I was fresh out of luck. The playground was deserted, meaning the bell had gone and everyone was already in class. I bit my lip, torn between taking the long way round or chancing the risky cut-through between the science and maths blocks. I checked my watch and decided to take a chance with the short-cut. It might be the hangout of choice for the class-skipping drop-outs of Year Eleven but I didn't want a detention staining my good-girl record. And maybe my luck would change and they'd be hanging out somewhere else for once.

At first glance, the path was empty. Sucking in a huge sigh of relief, I scurried into the gap. It wasn't until I was halfway down the path that a tell-tale waft of nicotine-laden smoke reached me and I knew I'd made a mistake. The path had appeared to be clear, but only because the usual suspects were loitering in an alcove by the back entrance of the science block, hidden from view. I hesitated. Now I had another dilemma; back up and go around the buildings or try to scoot past before their Neanderthal brains could fire off any insults. I had milliseconds to decide before the decision would be taken out of my hands.

'You're in the wrong place, short arse.' A mocking voice bounced off the walls and echoed along the path. 'The primary school is next door.'

Too late. As insults went I'd heard much worse, but I wasn't about to stop and give them comedy tips. My best chance now was to keep going and try to brazen it out. I glanced sideways as I drew level with them. The good news was that there were only four of them. The bad news was that the boys might only be a year older, but compared to dainty little me they looked like they'd just landed from Planet Hulk. I didn't recognise them but guessed they were the kind of kids the teachers had pretty much given up on.

'Nah, look at her, man,' one jeered as I hurried past. 'She ain't big enough to go to school. I bet she ain't even potty trained.'

They all laughed and I gritted my teeth, intending to keep on walking. I didn't want to speak, in case the lilt of my accent betrayed me as different. But they weren't letting me off so lightly. One of them, the biggest of the four, stepped out and grabbed the strap of my bag, yanking me backwards.

'Don't be ignoring us, little girl,' he growled, his tone geared up for maximum intimidation. 'We got a job for you.'

Every muscle tensed as adrenaline flooded through my body. *Run*, whispered my brain and I shot forwards, thinking the sudden movement would force him to let go. It didn't. Instead, he tightened his grip and almost jerked me off my feet. The handle of my bag stretched and creaked ominously as I struggled to stay upright. He dragged me towards him, an ugly sneer on his spot-covered face. Sour, smoke-ridden breath nearly made me gag as he spoke. 'You're gonna go down the shop and get us twenty fags.'

In spite of the gut-wrenching fear worming through my insides, I had to resist the temptation to roll my eyes at his monumental stupidity. Hadn't they just claimed I looked like I was still at primary school? So why would the bloke in the newsagent's think I was eighteen?

'Why can't you get them yourselves?' I said, hoping my voice wasn't as squeaky as it sounded, but I knew the answer already – they'd been banned for nicking.

Shrugging, he glanced at his mates. 'Why have a dog and bark yourself?'

Loud guffaws bounced off the red brick walls. It was hardly Edinburgh Fringe funny, but I didn't say so.

Instead, I leaned back to avoid another blast of stale breath. 'I can't. I'm too young.'

He twisted his hand around and connected hard with my shoulder. I thudded into the red brick wall and gasped as the air was forced from my lungs.

'Then you'd better grow up, fast. Because if you don't get us them cigarettes, we'll be waiting for you outside the school gates tonight.'

His nose was so close I could see the greasy filth blocking his pores. His mates loomed behind him, grinning and daring me to refuse. I stared at the ground, forcing my dully throbbing ribcage out of my mind and desperately searching for a way out. Sure, I could agree to get them what they wanted and then run as fast as I could to the school office, but that wouldn't stop them making my life a living hell. Kids like him had a thousand ways of inflicting misery without laying a finger on you. Verbal abuse hurt just as much and didn't leave any tell-tale bruises.

I looked up reluctantly, willing my eyes not to fill with tears. 'Look, I can't —'

A faint footstep in the alley made me stop. Then a low voice said, 'Let her go, Peterson.'

The words were laced with a veiled menace that sent a shiver down my spine. I craned my head to see who had spoken but the others were blocking my view. The boy pinning me to the wall twisted his head, scowling.

'This ain't nothing to do with you, man,' he snarled and I was surprised to detect a new note in his sullen voice. Fear? I wondered. Or respect?

The newcomer didn't seem to have heard. 'I said, let her go.'

You could have carved the atmosphere like a tree trunk. Around me, the boys shuffled restlessly, and I sensed they were preparing to fight. My heart pounded in my chest. I'd seen fights from a distance but that was all. What were my chances of scrambling clear once the fists started flying? And how would my rescuer, if that's what he was, cope with four against one?

The moment teetered on a knife edge. I tensed, ready to run, but then something shifted and it was like the battle had happened and I'd missed it. Either that or Peterson had decided I wasn't worth fighting over. In any case, he stepped backwards and yanked his hand roughly out of my bag handle, flashing an insincere grin my way. ''Course. We was only having a joke.'

The others took their lead from him and melted backwards. With a sneering jerk of his head, Peterson turned away and they sloped off down the alley. Shaken, I turned to thank my saviour, and for the second time that morning the breath whooshed out of me – only this time, I couldn't blame being pushed against the wall for my sudden breathlessness. Standing a few metres away was the most drop-dead gorgeous boy I'd ever seen. And he was staring at me with a chilling fascination. I drew in an unsteady breath as I stared back. No wonder Peterson had backed off without a fight; if I hadn't been practically paralysed by the beam of those smouldering eyes I would have wanted to run away too. Either that or go for the World's Longest Snog.

He was tall, even for a teenage boy; I felt like a doll in comparison. Tendrils of long fringe touched his eye-lashes and lay coal-like against his pale skin as he gazed at me with dark, heavy-lidded eyes. I was sure I'd never seen him before. With those devastating looks, I would definitely have remembered.

'Th-thanks,' I stuttered, hauling my bag up my arm self-consciously.

He studied me for a long moment before speaking. 'Don't cut through here again. It's asking for trouble.'

His black eyes raked over me again and then came to rest on my face. Shrinking under the weight of his gaze, I leaned against the wall for support. *This must be what a deer feels like just before the car hits*, my dazed brain whispered. Then, with one fluid movement, he brushed past me.

'I won't,' I called after him, for want of anything more intelligent to say. 'Thanks.'

He didn't show any sign of having heard. I watched him go, my breathing shallow as my heart slowed to its normal pace. Then I dragged my sleeve back and peered feverishly at my watch. Its hands weren't on my side; I was detention-inducingly late.

'Crap!' I muttered. Hauling my bag further on to my shoulder, I ran towards the main building. With a bit of luck I'd be in time to catch the end of registration. Panting, I pounded along the corridor and pushed back the door of my classroom. As I opened my mouth to mutter an apology, the tormented strap of my bag chose that moment to give up. My books, pencil case and a daintily wrapped sanitary towel spilled out across the floor and skittered to a halt in front of Mr Exton.

'Nice of you to join us, Miss Thackery,' he said, surveying the jumble before him and smiling humourlessly. 'That's a lunchtime detention you've just earned.'

Megan flashed me a sympathetic grimace, but the rest of my classmates sniggered. Face burning, I scrabbled everything back into my traitorous bag and slunk to my seat. Seriously, could this day get any worse?

Chapter 3

It could. And it did. Not only had I left my history coursework at home, I'd also forgotten to pick up any lunch money; not that I had any time to eat after I'd survived the hell that was lunchtime detention. I swear the teaching assistant supervising us knew Marcus Jones was flicking spit-balls at me, but she just buried her frizzy head in her book and ignored it.

So by the time I'd reached the last lesson of the day, my mood was once again blacker than a vampire's soul and the only thing keeping me going was the memory of my knight in shining armour that morning. The version of events running on loop in my head was only a little bit embellished; Peterson and his gang had their roles downgraded, obviously, and Mystery Boy was overcome with brooding admiration at my wit and fabulousness. I stared dreamily out of the RE classroom window, wondering who he was. I made up my mind to ask Megan later. Peterson had definitely known him, so maybe he was in Year Eleven. I really hoped he wasn't in the sixth form. It was a fact universally recognised that the sixth formers regarded the lower years as pond life.

Despite keeping an eye out as I'd moved from lesson to lesson, I hadn't seen Mystery Boy again. For one awful moment I wondered if he'd been a ghost, but then I remembered that Peterson had seen him too. Whoever he was, he'd got my attention big time, and in a way no other boy had come close to before.

Sister Margaret's voice was droning on in the background. We were supposedly learning about alternative religions, but half the class were texting and the rest had dozed off. It was hardly mind-blowing stuff, anyway; Sister Margaret was so hot for Christianity that she could hardly bring herself to mention any other religion. I studied her drab tweed skirt and fussy blouse dubiously; it wasn't a nun's habit, but there was no way you could mistake what she was. I didn't dare think about how she'd react if she ever found out what my aunt did for a living – spontaneously combust, probably, or report me to whatever the modern equivalent of the Witchfinder General was. I made a mental note that parents' evening was a definite no-no.

'Who can tell me about Buddhism?' Her bespectacled

gaze swept the room, searching for a victim. I glanced away a fraction too late, then made a frantic attempt to blend into the grubby beige walls. Her eyes gleamed and she pounced. 'Skye?'

I'd had a reputation as a bit of a boffin at my last school. It wasn't exactly something that had won me friends, so I'd made a conscious decision to dumb down during my first few weeks at Heath Park, at least until I'd got to know a few people. Sister Margaret wasn't doing me any favours. I considered sliding under the table, but nothing short of a medical emergency could save me now. Sighing inwardly, I dredged my memory for information.

'They believe all life is sacred and think that our souls are endlessly reincarnated.' My gaze narrowed as I thought some more. 'And they wear orange. A lot.'

Sister Margaret's mouth twisted into a humourless smile. 'Very good. Of course, Buddhism took most of its basic beliefs from Christianity, but they choose not to observe the divinity of our Lord.'

I relaxed into my seat, thinking she was about to launch into one of her rants about heaven and hell and the almighty Almighty. But she wasn't done with me.

'I don't believe you've shared your religious beliefs with us yet, Skye. Why don't you tell us about them now?'

Every molecule in my body froze. The class shifted in their seats and watched me with more interest than they'd shown in the rest of the lesson. I moistened my lips as my mind scrabbled furiously for an answer – whatever I said next, it couldn't be the truth. It wasn't that I didn't believe in God exactly, more that I'd seen enough ghosts to realise it was better to keep an open mind. I could hardly explain that to her now though. Should I take a chance on one of the mainstream world religions or was I better off going for atheism and bearing the brunt of Sister Margaret's barely concealed disdain? There were bound to be follow-up questions and what I knew about most religions could be written on a glamour model's bikini. Then I remembered something Jeremy had said a few nights ago as he'd forced me through another repeat of *Star Wars*.

'Did you know that Jedi is a proper religion?' he'd said, 'Thousands of people declared it on the population census a few years ago and since then it's grown worldwide.'

I'd shaken my head in disbelieving pity as he'd gone on to show a suspicious amount of knowledge about what sounded like the most crackpot belief system of the lot. But it was exactly what I needed to get Sister Margaret off my case. I was willing to bet my GHDs she wouldn't know where to begin with her questions. And it might just earn me a certain amount of begrudging respect among the other kids. OK, it would mostly be with the geeks, but I had to start somewhere . . .

Taking a deep breath, I took the plunge. 'I'm a Jedi, Sister Margaret. We believe that the infinite Force of the universe lies within everyone.'

There were gasps around the room and barely muffled laughter broke out in the rows behind me. Sister Margaret's jaw dropped as she stared at me, revealing ugly dark grey fillings on her back teeth. It was a full ten seconds before she pulled herself together enough to close her mouth. 'You dare to mock me?'

It was my turn to be stunned. 'No. It's a genuine religion.'

'It ridicules everything true faith stands for,' she snapped, her eyes narrowing in fury. 'People have died for their beliefs and you sit there and tell me you are a member of a church based on make-believe?'

I could have argued. What was the Bible but a collection of stories? But I knew it was pointless. Just like I knew exactly what was coming next.

'Get to the head teacher's office.' Fixing me with a steel gaze, she pointed a dramatic finger at the door. 'You clearly need to consider the state of your soul and you can do it in —'

'Detention, yes, I know,' I cut in, getting to my feet dispiritedly. What was that old saying; it never rained but it poured? I'd never really understood it before, but at that moment it felt like I had my own personal thunder cloud right above my head.

As I reached the door, the nun fired her parting shot. 'I'll pray for you, my child.'

I didn't slam the door, even though a voice in my head was screaming to. With extreme care, I pulled it closed and squeezed my eyelids down in miserable rage. Celestine and Jeremy were doing their best to help me settle in, but nothing was working out. I'd gone my whole school life without a detention and now I had two in the same day. My new teachers seemed to be determined to make my life as awful as possible, and I'd become a bully-magnet. Oh yeah, and a sixteenth century witch was giving me fashion tips. If I didn't know better I'd suspect someone had stolen my actual life and replaced it with the crappiest one they could find. For the first time I wondered if I'd made a mistake letting my mum go to Australia. How was I supposed to get through another three days of this, let alone the next two years?

As I trudged towards the head teacher's office, I knew I was sinking into Self-Pity City but I couldn't help myself. At least at my old school I'd had a few mates to knock about with. At Heath Park, everyone had their friends already and no one except Megan had room for a slightly off-the-wall midget who wasn't exactly cheer-leader material. On paper I sounded OK – blue eyes, wavy blond hair and a dusting of freckles on my upturned nose. But once you threw in a tendency to squint into the distance a lot (especially if I'd run out of contact lenses) and a habit of talking to people no one else could see, maybe you'll understand why I wasn't winning any popularity contests.

Feeling totally sorry for myself, I rounded the corner and was halfway across the hallway that led to the closed door of the head teacher's PA's office when a shout rang out behind me.

'You, girl! Stop!'

The voice had the ominous ring of authority. My shoulders slumped. For crying out loud, how many more teachers were going to tell me off today?

I stopped and turned slowly. And relaxed. Unless Heath Park had a weird recruitment policy, the teacher I was looking at wasn't a current member of staff. If the glowing blue outline hadn't given him away, the fact that he was hovering several centimetres off the ground would have done. On top of that, his grey suit looked like something my great-granddad would've worn. In fact, with his waxed handlebar moustache and yellow-checked bow tie, he might have stepped straight from the pages of a World War II propaganda poster.

'Are you talking to me?' I asked uncertainly. It was entirely possible he'd been yelling at some ghostly student I hadn't seen.

'Of course I'm talking to you!' he roared, his bushy eyebrows burrowing into one another ferociously. 'Although I must say it's a pleasant surprise to have one of you little blighters actually listen for once.'

He must have been a past teacher at the school, I guessed, who'd somehow died on the job. From the way he was dressed it had been a long time ago. I felt a tiny stab of sympathy as I imagined him being surrounded by kids who didn't pay him the blindest bit of notice. Then again, wasn't that kind of what teaching was like now?

'Sorry, sir,' I said, deciding it made sense to humour him. He might not be exactly like the rest of the teachers at Heath Park, but he could still make my life a misery if I crossed him.

He eyed me beadily. 'It's Dr Bailey to you. Why aren't you in class?'

'I've been sent to the head teacher, sir.'

His face creased into a forbidding frown. 'I see. For what reason, may I ask?'

A faint rustle echoed from beyond the curve of the corridor behind him. I glanced over his shoulder uneasily, aware that I appeared to be having a conversation with Mr Nobody. When you were psychic, it went with the territory, but I'd prefer it if no one heard.

Distracted, I stepped closer to him and lowered my voice. 'I told Sister Margaret I was a Jedi.'

His eyebrows shot upwards. 'A what? Speak up, child, I can barely hear you.'

I peered into the corridor, gnawing my lip in anxiety. Was there someone there or not? 'She asked about religion,' I stage-whispered. 'I could hardly tell her the truth, could I?'

'Which is?'

Tilting my head to one side, I stared at him. 'I talk to dead people. What do you think my religious beliefs might be?'

He drew himself up to his full height. 'Heresy!' he boomed. 'Write out one hundred times, *I must not blaspheme* and report back to me tomorrow morning.'

This can't be happening, I decided with an inward groan. Of all the ghosts in all the world, I'd found one who didn't believe in, well – himself. Next, he'd be telling me he wasn't dead, he was just between bodies, but this wasn't the time or the place for a conversation like that. 'Yes, sir.'

He turned on his heel and stalked away. Before I could start on my way to the head's office again there was another, louder rustle in the corridor.

'Who's there?' I called.

For a moment I thought I'd imagined it. Then I heard the unmistakable clatter of footsteps heading my way and knew they were too close for me to escape being seen. I stood glued to the spot in the exposed hall, running my conversation with the ghost through my head. Whoever was coming had potentially heard every word I'd said. How in the name of Yoda was I going to explain that away?

Chapter 4

Is there some unwritten law of the universe which says whatever can go wrong, will go wrong? If there isn't, I'd have to invent one. Because when the eavesdropper stepped into the hallway, I was plunged into a maelstrom of simultaneous ecstasy and embarrassment. Of all the people who could have witnessed my spook-tastic encounter, it had to be – just had to be – Mystery Boy. As the emotions slugged it out inside me, my old friend Sinking Dread joined the party when I realised Mystery Boy was staring at me like I'd just landed from Planet Nutjob. Great. Once he'd told all his mates what he'd heard, how long would it be before everyone was looking at me that way?

Once again, my powers of conversation seemed to be on a day trip away from my brain. 'You.'

He studied me, his features unmoving, and even in the depths of my humiliation, I noticed that eerie stillness extended throughout his body. It was almost as though he was poised to pounce on me at any second. A sly voice in my head whispered that I wouldn't mind so much if he did.

'Who were you talking to?' he asked in a level voice.

The darkness of his stare was hypnotic. I shook off the temptation to lose myself in the inky depths and glanced around guiltily. 'No one.'

His gaze didn't waver as he raised an eyebrow. 'You were. I heard you.'

I kicked my misfiring brain for a decent reply. It wasn't giving me much to work with. In fact, it seemed overwhelmingly preoccupied with pouting at the sex god in front of me. Plausible reasons for my peculiar behaviour were in short supply.

Feeling my cheeks begin to stain pink, I grabbed the only option I had, ignoring the screeching protest of my mind. 'Um . . . I was talking to . . . myself.'

'Yourself?' His voice dripped with suspicion and I could hardly blame him. For a one-way conversation I'd been pretty animated. 'What are you, schizophrenic or something?'

Eek. The part of me that wanted to inflict death by snogging let out a despairing cry, but the sensible part realised that a bona fide mental illness sounded way more believable than the truth. I was just glad he couldn't see my aura. 'Yeah. Actually, it's time for, er, my medication, so I should go.'

He watched me in silence again and I stared back, my heart thudding with fear. At least I assumed that's what it was; it might also have been love.

'Medication, right,' he said, drawling out the words in evident disbelief. 'Only I thought I heard you say something about dead people.'

Panic clutched at my already churning stomach. 'I didn't. Isn't it funny how sound gets distorted in these old buildings?' My nervy giggle seemed squeaky and shrill over the rushing noise in my ears. 'Anyway, my medicine is kept in the nurse's room.' I waved a hand towards the offices behind me and edged backwards. 'So . . . um . . . I'd better . . . make like a tree.'

Cheeks burning with excruciating embarrassment, I fled.

'Wait!' he called, but I pretended not to hear. As I scurried towards the relative safety of the head teacher's office I could feel him watching me. I didn't dare to look back. *Make like a tree?* Had I really just said that? I hadn't even delivered the punchline – *and leave.* In fact, I couldn't have been more of a loser if I'd had an enormous L tattooed on my forehead. But even more sickening than my Daisy Dork routine was the horrible feeling that Mystery Boy hadn't believed a word I'd said. I couldn't decide which was worse; mental illness wasn't exactly a turn-on in a girl, but neither was the truth. Either way, if Mystery Boy talked, I was sunk. The question was, how far?

'No need to ask how your day went,' Celestine said when I slouched through the door after school.

'Don't tell me,' I said, pausing to sniff the flowers she was arranging on the hall table. 'My aura is filthy black.'

'Not quite, but it's pretty close. I'd say cowpat brown. Want to tell me about it?'

Charming, I thought, and considered her offer. Could I bear to go through what was officially the crappiest day of my life again? OK, I'd met the most gorgeous boy in the galaxy, but he thought I was a complete fruit-loop. Would she have any idea how exhilarated and nauseous I felt inside? I watched her fuss over the angle of a disobedient lily and wondered if she'd ever been through the same thing; maybe, but it still didn't make me feel like baring my soul.

'Not really,' I said, puffing my fringe out of my eyes. 'Although I should probably mention that the head teacher is going to call to discuss my "inappropriate sense of humour".'

My mum would have flipped. Celestine merely lifted an eyebrow. It made me want to hug her. 'Oh?'

I didn't elaborate. 'And do you have any idea how I go about writing lines for a ghost?'

Now both eyebrows were raised. 'With paper and a pen, I imagine. Are you sure you don't want to talk?'

'Talk about what?' Jeremy wandered in from the living room and looked questioningly from Celestine to me. 'Problems at school?'

If Celestine couldn't help, I doubted Jeremy could. What I really needed was to get online so I could tap into the hive mind of MSN and work out what to do next. But I'd kept my psychic ability a closely guarded secret back in Edinburgh and my mates wouldn't know a thing about Mystery Boy. The person I needed to speak to was Megan. 'It's nothing,' I said, shaking my head in Jeremy's direction. 'Forget it.'

Concern crinkled his forehead and he reached out to touch my arm. 'You might think we're practically OAPs, but we are here to help, you know.'

I stared at his sympathetic expression, wondering what he thought he could do. He wasn't fully psychic like my aunt and me so he couldn't really understand what it was like to live with the dead on a daily basis. And he definitely wasn't any help in the coolness stakes; were those actual corduroy trousers he was wearing? Then I dragged my gaze upwards and saw the glitter of compassion in his eyes. He meant well, and his crimes against fashion were nothing a trip to the shops wouldn't fix; maybe I'd give up my lie-in one Saturday and educate him. Dredging up a crooked smile, I said, 'Thanks, but I think this is something I need to deal with on my own.'

He took the hint and changed the subject. 'How about a trip to the theatre with me tonight? We've got a comedian doing a month-long run and he's not half bad.'

It was a definite perk of Jeremy's job as a lighting engineer at an old West End theatre that he could take occasional visitors along. I'd been a few times already, and despite rumours of a theatre ghost, I'd been blissfully undisturbed throughout the performances. A night of laughter was exactly what I needed. I opened my mouth to say so but my aunt got there before me.

'Sorry, Jeremy, I have other plans for Skye tonight.'

It was news to me. 'What plans?'

She shrugged apologetically. 'I hadn't got round to telling you about it yet. Why don't we go and sit down and I'll explain?'

Fighting the urge to pull out my phone and fire off a text to Megan, I followed her into the living room and perched on the dark leather sofa, wondering what Celestine had planned. I really hoped it didn't involve Mary; she was taking annoying to a whole new level and had started to hide my make-up bag every morning. Our relationship was colder than Frosty the Snowman's armpit and, not for the first time, I wished she'd find someone else to haunt.

Celestine jumped straight in. 'There's a ghost who's been hanging around at the Dearly D for about a week now. He never speaks and leaves whenever we try to approach him. I think he wants help, but he doesn't trust us.'

I wasn't surprised. It wasn't unusual for ghosts to find unconventional ways to get attention, which explained why poltergeists existed. The extreme violence they displayed usually stemmed from a deep-seated rage, but often it was a cry for help. Once a psychic was able to communicate with them and uncover the reason for the anger, they were on the road to helping the ghost to move on. It was why the Church of the Dearly Departed was so popular among both the living and the dead – it was the place you went to get answers. Even when you didn't have the faintest clue what the question was.

I could see where my aunt was heading. 'So you want me to try and talk to him.' Thinking for a minute, I added, 'What makes you think he won't run from me too?'

Her smile was gentle. 'He's around your age, maybe a bit older than you. If you can find out a bit about him, perhaps we can help.'

If he was anything like most teenage boys I'd be lucky to get a grunt out of him, but I didn't say that. Then again, maybe dying young had given him a good reason to distrust the world.

Jeremy shifted on the sofa beside me and I guessed he

must be thinking about Lucy, the teenage ghost he'd helped to pass across the year before. She'd been trapped in a toilet on Carnaby Street until Jeremy had arrived and helped her to escape. It had been his one and only psychic experience and although he admitted he'd been terrified at first, he'd also seen how much she needed someone to listen. So he'd stuck around. Without him, she'd still be there – lonely, scared and bored out of her mind. I couldn't imagine how she'd felt, but the ghost at the Dearly D must know. A stab of pity cut into me and I came to a sudden decision; no one deserved a fate like that. Whoever he was, I'd do what I could to help.

'OK,' I said. 'What time do we need to leave?'

My aunt looked pleased. 'Around six.'

Leaning back into the sofa, I reached towards the laptop on the coffee table. 'Excellent, so I've got time to go on Facebook?'

Celestine got to her feet. 'Of course,' she said as she headed out of the room. 'But ghostly lines don't write themselves.'

I prised open the screen and stuck my tongue out at her retreating back.

'If the wind changes it'll stay like that,' she called, without turning round.

As I slumped back into my seat, Jeremy grinned at me. 'I don't know how she does it either. Maybe Mary's been teaching her witchcraft.'

The way Celestine was acting, I wouldn't have been surprised if it was the other way around.

Typically, Megan wasn't online. One or two friends from Edinburgh were on MSN, though, and we chatted for a while, but Megan's name didn't pop up in my chat window before Celestine demanded I log off. I swallowed my frustration; Mystery Boy's identity would have to wait.

It had been dark a full hour by the time we got to the Dearly D, but the chilly February night didn't put anyone off coming to the service. As usual, there was a crowd outside the entrance, but to the average passer-by, the pavement looked pretty empty. I nodded to a few of the regulars, both the living and the faintly glowing dead, as we went inside. Sometimes we saw the same faces for months on end before we found a way to help them, sometimes they were gone much more quickly. But even the newest arrivals soon learned to respect the privacy of the psychics who worked there and never approached them outside of the service for help. So, although there were plenty of waves and nods as we made our way down the aisle to the front of the church, no one stood in our way. I didn't see anyone matching the description of the ghost I was there to help.

'Where does he usually sit?' I asked Celestine once

we'd greeted the other psychics and taken our seats at the bottom of the altar steps.

'It varies,' she said. 'He's sat in the middle pews once or twice, but most of the time he stays at the back.'

When I'd been younger, I'd wondered why ghosts didn't just sink through furniture. Celestine had explained that the habits of their physical existence were so engrained that most people stuck with them even after their death. So they tended not to zoom around the ceiling and treated the world pretty much like they had when they were alive. They regularly walked through walls, of course, but who wouldn't? It had to be easier than opening doors. 'And he never speaks?'

'Not even to the younger ghosts. I'm hoping that he'll spot you and feel able to open up.'

It was as likely as hell freezing over, but I nodded and scanned the church. The pews were filling up but teenagers were few and far between. Maybe Celestine was right and all Mr Distrustful needed was a friendly face his own age to talk to. I didn't have much else to offer him.

It wasn't until the service was in full swing that I felt Celestine nudge me. I glanced over and she tilted her head fractionally towards the left of the church. My gaze roved along the rows of the living and the dead until it came to rest on one ghost in particular. Younger than most of the congregation, he was slouched in an empty pew, his hood up and arms folded. Even from a distance I could see the look of sullen distrust on his black face. If he'd still had an aura it would have screamed, 'Get lost'.

He caught me staring. Feeling as though I'd somehow been intruding, I fought the instinct to look away and instead offered him the tiniest of smiles. He didn't return it, just stared back at me and raised his chin in mute challenge. So, that was how he wanted to play it – a staring match, the first to blink or look away being the loser. Without breaking eye contact, I settled back in my seat; I'd played this game a hundred times before at my old school, although admittedly never against a ghost, who wouldn't have the disadvantage of feeling their eyes turning into pickled onions. But he was offering me a way to win his respect so I ignored the twitching in my eyelids and matched his dead-eye stare.

Seconds ticked past and turned into minutes. Then, just as I reached the point where I thought my eyes were going to burst out of my head with the pressure, he looked away. I slumped in my seat and blinked frantically, while the service carried on oblivious around us. When I opened my eyes again, the ghost was heading towards the back of the church. I shifted in my seat but Celestine laid a discreet hand on my arm.

'We'll be breaking for individual consultations in a minute,' she murmured. 'Go after him then.'

Fiddling with the zip on my jacket, I waited. What if I'd misread the signs and he was out of sight by the time I got outside? I'd have missed my chance and he might not give me another one.

I needn't have worried. He was waiting for me in the cold night air, leaning on a low brick wall opposite the church and pretending he wasn't watching the door. The street-light flickered on and off, making the soft luminosity around the ghost more noticeable. I hesitated for a nanosecond, trying to work out a plan, then decided I'd have to wing it. Thrusting my hands into my pockets, I crossed the empty road and stopped about a metre away.

'All right?' I said, injecting casual indifference into my voice while wondering whether he was going to answer.

He stared down at the ground for a full minute before he replied. 'S'up?'

I let out the breath I'd been holding. If he'd ignored me it would have been game over. 'Not much. I've just come out for some fresh air. It gets proper stuffy in there.'

A frown furrowed his forehead. 'You're not from round here.'

'I'm from Edinburgh. I've just moved down.'

The silence stretched between us, but it wasn't up to me to break it. We were playing by his rules and instinct told me it was his move. Sure enough, after a few more seconds he spoke again. 'You one of them psychics?'

'Yeah.'

He looked at me then, his face a mixture of resentment and curiosity. 'It must be well weird, seeing dead people everywhere. I never even knew they was there, before I died.'

You and the rest of the world, I thought. 'I've always been able to see them. You get used to it after a while.' I gave a tiny laugh. 'I was best mates with one when I was really little.'

A look of surprise crossed his face. 'For real?'

'She was called Poppy. I talked to her all the time. Everyone thought she was an imaginary friend. It wasn't until my aunt came to visit and saw us together that my mum found out the truth.'

And practically had a fit when she realised I was psychic, but I didn't mention that part. She'd calmed down over the years, but I don't think she ever got over the shock of realising I had the gift when she didn't.

'So your aunt sees ghosts as well?' He studied me for a moment, then waved a hand at the church. 'Was that her in there?'

I nodded.

'You look like family,' he said. 'But your mum isn't psychic?'

'No.' I decided that whatever game we'd been playing

was over now and it was OK to introduce myself. 'I'm Skye Thackery.'

'Dontay Ambrose.' He held out a fist and I tried to tap it with my own. My fingers slid through his and I dropped my hand with a shiver.

Now that we were on first-name terms, I guessed it was all right to sit next to him on the wall. It looked more natural to passers-by than me standing on my own in the middle of the pavement. Not that anyone had walked past, but I didn't want to risk attracting the wrong kind of attention. In somewhere like Kensal Green any sort of attention could be the wrong kind. 'Are you, er, from round here?'

'Nah,' he replied, throwing a scornful look up and down the street. 'Kensal Green is small time, man. I'm from Hackney.'

I stared at him. Where had I heard that name recently? Then a memory surfaced. 'A boy got really badly beaten there last week. I saw it on the news.'

Dontay's eyes didn't meet mine. 'Yeah, and?'

'It was a gang crime, wasn't it?' I heard my tone hardening at his apparent indifference. 'He was on another gang's turf so they taught him a lesson.'

He shrugged, but it wasn't convincing. 'You got to be careful round there. They don't tolerate no disrespect.'

The cogs in my brain whirred. 'So you were a gang member?'

A closed look came over his face and his gaze skittered away. 'Might have been.'

The mixed messages I was getting were confusing. On one hand, he seemed almost proud of where he was from, but on the other, I'd sensed hostility towards the gang culture which seemed to be part of his everyday life there. Hesitantly, I asked, 'Is that how you died?'

He pushed off from the wall with a violent effort, facing me angrily. 'What's it to you how I died? I didn't come here for no interrogation.'

He turned and stormed off down the street, passing a group of men heading towards me.

'Dontay, wait!' I started to call, but the words died in my throat. From the way the men were staggering along it looked like they'd spent the afternoon in the pub and their slurred conversation was drifting along the pavement. The last thing I needed was a drunken run-in. With a dejected shrug, I gave up on Dontay and headed back to the Dearly D. I hoped he'd be back once he'd calmed down, because underneath the attitude, I'd seen a flash of how he really felt: scared and alone. Sooner or later he'd have to admit he needed help. And until that happened, at least I had his name.

Chapter 5

On Wednesday morning I had to catch the bus because Mary had hidden one of my shoes, and by the time I'd found it I didn't have time to walk. The downside of it was that I was treated to a glimpse of the suicide ghost as we trundled over Hornsey Lane Bridge. Watching her tortured face through the window as we rolled by, I decided I'd take Jeremy up on his offer of a lift. Apart from anything else, I was starting to dread my journey to school each day.

It was turning out to be harder than I expected to find out who the woman was. Once Celestine and I had got back from the Dearly D, I'd been straight on to the laptop, hoping to catch Megan on MSN, but there was no sign of her. Then I remembered she'd mentioned going to the cinema with her parents and younger sister.

None of my Edinburgh friends were online either; MSN was so quiet it practically had tumbleweeds blowing across the screen. I'd spent the rest of the evening Googling both our mystery ghosts. Although I couldn't find the woman I'd seen, there were plenty of other suicides in Highgate to choose from, and they made grim reading. I shuddered in bleak disbelief as we scrolled through report after report of the desperate souls who'd leaped to their deaths from the bridge at Hornsey Lane.

'I so need to find another way to school,' I said to Celestine as we read on. 'That bridge is seriously bad news.'

She nodded. 'I've driven underneath it once or twice and got a chill each time. I try to avoid it if I can.'

Google had more to offer when I tapped in *Dontay Ambrose*, but in a way I wished it hadn't. He was from the estates that towered over the Hackney skyline, and his story had made the headlines for all the wrong reasons. I understood why he'd kicked off when I'd asked about gangs. Although the newspaper reports claimed he was one of the London Fields Posse, he hadn't died because of it. In fact, his heartbroken mother had sworn he'd hated the violent culture around him, which explained his reaction to my questions. Hanging with a mate outside the tall block of flats where he'd lived, Dontay had been caught in the crossfire of a drive-by shooting. Paramedics had struggled to stem the bleeding from the wounds to his thigh and neck, but he hadn't really stood a chance. It had been a tragic consequence of a pointless war; being in the wrong place at the wrong time had cost him his life. No wonder he was angry.

I approached the school gates with an odd mixture of anticipation and uneasiness swirling around with my Coco Pops. If Mystery Boy had blabbed to his mates, I might as well turn around and go home because, by now, the entire school probably knew I was mentally unhinged. If he had, it wouldn't really matter what I did next; the whispering would have already begun.

As I crossed the playground, I braced myself for the onslaught of muttered comments and averted looks. Dr Bailey was there, glowering at the other kids. 'You there! Smarten up or ship out, boy!'

I had his lines in my bag, thanks to Jeremy's genius idea of typing them up using one of the handwriting fonts on the laptop. It'd taken minutes to do and Dr Bailey would be none the wiser. He'd have to wait until lessons had begun, though; I couldn't risk being caught apparently talking to myself again. I ducked out of his line of sight, my eyes darting left and right for evidence that I was the hot topic on the gossip grapevine. There didn't seem to be any. A group of Year Sevens giggled when I walked by, but that didn't mean anything – giggling came as standard with them. In fact, as I reached registration without a single thing out of the ordinary happening, I realised it could only mean one thing: Mystery Boy hadn't told.

Typically, there was no sign of Megan, so I joined the end of the queue outside the classroom and leaned against the corridor wall. One or two of the other kids nodded to me, and Ellie McCauley threw me a dirty look, but there was no smothered laughter and definitely no pointing. I couldn't believe my luck; anyone else would have spread it over Facebook faster than you could say 'freak show'. Of course, there was always the chance that he was ill and that the true horror would hit me the next day, but I'd worry about that later. What mattered right now was getting through today.

Mr Exton was late, an irony that wasn't lost on me. I was idly dreaming about handing him a lunchtime detention when I realised a furious whispering had broken out among Ellie and her mates. Here it comes, I thought, misery uncoiling in my gut; the nightmare begins. But judging from the excited glances they were casting along the corridor behind me, I wasn't the topic of conversation. It had to be someone pretty high up the Heath Park pecking order to send the McCauley Coven into such a frenzy. I twisted round and craned my head to see what the fuss was about, but since I was pretty much the shortest fourteen-year-old on the planet, my chances were zero.

'Hi, Nico,' I heard Ellie simper and I followed her gaze. My jaw dropped open in disbelief. For the third time in two days, I was looking at Mystery Boy. Was he stalking me or something?

He wasn't returning Ellie's admiring glances, though. His eyes were fixed on me, dark and intense. His expression was unfathomable as he slowed.

'All right?' he said, raising his chin in greeting.

I nodded, my tongue suddenly feeling twice its size and incapable of speech. Then he was past me and disappearing along the corridor. My frazzled brain scrambled to catch up. He wasn't off sick, which had to mean he'd kept quiet about my little 'episode' the day before. As grateful as I was, I couldn't help wondering why.

'Who was that?' I demanded of Ellie.

Peering after him, she didn't reply. Megan did, though. I hadn't even noticed her arrive.

'Nico Albescu, from the other half of Year Ten,' she said breathlessly, her eyes glittering with interest. 'Man of mystery and officially the Fittest Boy Ever.'

So how come she hadn't mentioned him before? I'd heard plenty about Charlie Henderson, who Megan had admired from afar since Year Eight, but nothing about a solid gold hottie in our midst. 'Albescu?' I echoed, frowning. 'What kind of surname is that – Polish?'

Megan's forehead creased as she stared after him.

'Romanian, but I think he's lived in this country most of his life, because his English is so good. He started here in September and keeps himself to himself. Disappears every now and then, which is why you haven't seen him before. Single, as far as we know.'

Ellie turned round and studied me through narrowed eyes. 'He seems to know you, though. How? You've only been here five minutes and he doesn't bother with just anyone.'

I shrugged. 'I've bumped into him a few times, that's all.'

She looked like she didn't believe a word of it. 'Don't get any ideas about him. He's mine.'

'Has anyone told him that?' I said, before my survival instinct cut in.

Ellie's pretty face darkened with jealousy as she stepped towards me. 'You're new, so I'm going to pretend I didn't hear that, but I mean it when I say keep away from him. This isn't *High School Musical* and Little Miss Geeky does not steal the show. Get it?'

In other circumstances I might have risen to the challenge, but I couldn't get involved with Nico Albescu. So what if he went right up to eleven on the gorgeousness scale and had swooped in like Prince Charming's sexier younger brother? Even if I did owe him for keeping quiet about the incident in the hallway it didn't mean we were going to be mates. Or anything else, no matter how much he turned my brain to jelly and made my stomach flip whenever I saw him. Because the simple truth was that I'd never trusted anyone with my secret, not even my closest friends back in Scotland. How did you begin a conversation like that? Maybe one day I'd meet someone I could confide in, but they'd have to be pretty special or I'd be checking in at Heartbreak Hotel before I knew it.

Mr Exton turned up and huffed his way to the front of the line to open the classroom. I couldn't explain the real reason I couldn't be interested in Nico to Ellie, but if I wanted to save myself some unnecessary grief I'd have to show her I wasn't a threat. As I sank into my seat I could practically hear her sharpening her claws.

While Mr Exton called the register from his laptop, I peered down at my timetable. Ellie and I hardly shared any of the same classes but we did have PE together that afternoon. Maybe I'd get a chance to talk to her then, preferably before she decapitated me with a hockey stick.

Megan twisted in her seat and leaned towards me. 'Don't worry about Ellie. She's fancied Nico since he arrived, but he doesn't even know she exists.' She pushed her Calvin Klein glasses back up her nose and grinned. 'Which is why she got so bothered when he spoke to you. How do you know him?'

'I don't really,' I murmured back. 'He sorted out a few

Year Eleven boys who were having a go yesterday, but that's about it.'

It wasn't exactly the whole truth, but it was enough for Megan. Her eyes widened. 'He rescued you?' she squeaked. 'How romantic!'

Mr Exton looked up in irritation and Megan spun round to face the front. I stared at her mass of chestnut curls and thought about what she'd said. Now that she mentioned it, I supposed it did sound kind of romantic, but the reality had been anything but; my bruised ribcage was proof of that. And although Nico had appeared out of nowhere to save me, he'd hardly stuck around afterwards to sweep me off my feet. No, I decided, romance had definitely not featured highly.

The second Mr Exton's attention was back on the laptop, Megan twisted round again, her eyes gleaming with excitement. 'Did you exchange longing glances? Ellie is going to go nuts when she finds out!'

Longing glances? Where was this girl from – Mills and Boonsville? 'No, we didn't, and I'd rather Ellie didn't find out about it.' Her face lit up and I knew I'd said the wrong thing. 'Not that there's anything to find out about. Nico appeared, Peterson and his gang left and we all went our separate ways. End of story.'

Well, almost end of story, I thought as I crossed my fingers under the table.

'*Except* that he came to find you this morning.'

I sighed. 'No, he happened to walk past me in the corridor.'

Megan shook her head from side to side like a wet dog. 'He didn't. The other Year Ten classes are over on the opposite side of the building so he had no reason to be here.' She paused meaningfully. 'Other than searching for you, that is.'

Mr Exton's head rose sharply and his expression was one of extreme annoyance. 'Do you girls want to share your conversation with the rest of the class, since it clearly can't wait until breaktime?'

Eek, absolutely not. Megan faced the front and we both chorused, 'No, sir.'

We sat in silence until the bell rang for first lesson. As we left the room, Megan mouthed, 'Lunchtime!' at me. I nodded and headed off to double science. Next time I saw her I was going to have to set her straight. There was nothing happening between Nico and me. It was a non-story.

Chapter 6

My relationship with my mum is what you might call complicated. Don't get me wrong, I love her dearly and I know she feels the same way about me, but I always felt things changed once she knew I was psychic. It's like I was in a gang she could never join, and that somehow made her feel differently towards me. On the outside she was still the same loving mother she'd always been, kissing my knees better when I fell over and putting on funny voices to read my bedtime stories, but I'd occasionally catch her watching me as though she didn't really know me at all. When she'd been offered the chance to study in Australia, I knew that a tiny part of her wanted a chance at normality, and that had hurt. She was still my mother, whatever our problems were, and my only living parent. But although

I hadn't wanted her to go, it was an opportunity of a lifetime and I couldn't stand in her way. In spite of our differences, I still missed her every day. We spoke on the phone loads, but even a webcam wasn't enough to bridge the distance sometimes.

Celestine was doing her best to make it up to me. Since I'd moved in with her, we'd grown closer than ever and I knew she could read how much I missed Mum. Maybe that was why she'd suggested my helping out at the Dearly D.

'Fancy coming to work with me again later?' she asked as I sat at the breakfast bar on Thursday evening, puzzling over negative fractions. 'I'm hoping Dontay will be back.'

I thought about it. From the way he'd freaked out last time I wasn't at all sure he'd show up again, but if he did, I wanted to be there. I'd breezed through my homework, and, miraculously, there'd been no more run-ins with the teachers, ghostly or otherwise. I didn't want to jinx anything, but it felt like things were finally starting to settle down. Maybe I could juggle my social life and psychic life after all. 'Yeah, OK.'

'It might be better if you don't ask him straight out about his death. Let him tell you about it in his own time.'

I nodded as I polished off the last equation. I'd figured that much out for myself. As much as I wanted to help Dontay, I wasn't going to make the mistake of over-stepping the boundary again. Which only left the problem of what we *were* going to talk about. Somehow, I didn't think *Gossip Girl* was going to cut it.

I spotted him as soon as we walked in, and this time he didn't bother with the staring match. Waiting until Celestine had discreetly melted away, he approached me, hands stuffed in his pockets and head down.

'Hey,' I said when he shuffled to a stop at the front of the church. 'How've you been?'

'All right,' he mumbled, still staring down at the red-carpeted floor. Then he looked up. 'Apart from being dead, obviously.'

I grinned and the tension between my shoulder blades eased. 'Yeah, apart from that.'

He flashed me an apologetic look. 'I'm sorry I went off the other night.'

'It's OK. I was being nosey anyway.'

A smile tugged at his lips. 'Maybe a bit.'

Glancing around at the rapidly filling church, I said, 'Do you want to go somewhere to talk? They've got some rooms here and I don't really want to stand outside looking like a lunatic again.'

A wary expression crept over his face. 'S'pose.'

'Unless you'd rather chat to some of the other ghosts? Mrs Peacock would love to tell you about her varicose veins.'

He shuddered. 'Nah. Let's get out of here.'

We slipped through the vestry door and into one of the small side rooms Celestine had told me would be empty. The rooms were set up for the psychics to meet with bereaved families and most had comfortable chairs and a low table. I flicked the light on and settled into a flowery armchair, tucking my legs underneath me. Dontay sat on the sofa in silence, looking like he wished he was somewhere else.

I wiped my clammy palms on my jeans. 'This is a bit strange,' I ventured, as much to break the ice as anything. 'Although it's probably weirder for you than me. I mean, I've been talking to ghosts my whole life but you've only been dead . . .' I trailed off, waiting for him to fill in the blanks.

For a second, I thought he wouldn't answer. Then he cleared his throat. 'Four months. It feels a lot longer, though.'

I glanced around the room, with its vase of wilting flowers on the chipped coffee table and faded yellow curtains at the window. Ancient magazines fanned out across the ring-marked surface between us. It was like a cross between an old people's home and a doctor's surgery, and I couldn't imagine a worse place to sit with someone who didn't totally trust you. How was he ever going to open up if neither of us was comfortable?

My gaze came to rest on the football shirt peeking out from underneath his hoodie. I didn't recognise the colours, but the glimmer of an idea popped into my head. Celestine probably wouldn't approve, but I was getting nowhere fast. 'Do you want to get out of here?'

'Where to?' He stood up and followed me into the hallway.

'Back to my house. Unless you've got a better idea?'

Dontay shook his head and threw me a relieved grin. 'Nah, I'm happy to go. This reminds me of my nan's place.'

There was a strange, musty pong coming from the room. Hurriedly, I pulled the door closed. 'Then let's go. I think the England match is on telly tonight.'

His face lit up and I knew I'd scored. 'What are we waiting for?' he said eagerly. 'It'll be kicking off soon.'

There was a door at the end of the corridor which led out on to the street. It was supposed to be for emergencies only, but I didn't want to risk getting caught up in the spiritualist service and losing my chance with Dontay. Tapping out a quick text to Celestine to tell her where we'd gone, I hoped she'd understand. She'd never brought her work home and I was pretty sure I wasn't supposed to either, but surely getting Dontay to confide in me was the important thing. Wasn't it?

Dontay coped with the Underground surprisingly well. He'd refused to run after me for the train, though. As the doors closed and we juddered forwards, I thought I'd lost him. Then he'd coolly stepped off the platform and into the carriage, flashing me a knowing grin as he sussed I'd been worried.

The match had just started as we flicked on the TV. Jeremy was at work so I knew we'd have the plasma screen all to ourselves, which was just as well considering the amount of instructions Dontay was bellowing at the players. England were already winning one-nil, but he was still throwing his arms up in despair at every missed tackle.

'So you like football, then?' I ventured during a momentary lull when the ball went out of play.

His eyes didn't leave the screen. 'Yeah, we're a West Ham family through and through.' He blinked and a subdued look crept across his face. 'Or we were.'

We watched in silence for a moment. England had the ball and were pushing forwards. Mum and I had never been big on sport, but I hoped Dontay didn't expect me to cheer England on; my Scottish ancestors would have flocked from the astral plane to give me a piece of their minds.

'Did you play?'

He nodded. 'I wasn't bad, either. I even got scouted by the West Ham Youth Academy.'

As little as I know about football, even I knew that being scouted for a team like that was a pretty big deal.

Impressed, I said, 'You must have been good to get picked up by them.'

A wry grin tugged at his lips. 'Nelson was better than me. I'd never tell him that, mind.'

'Nelson?'

'My kid brother,' he explained. His attention flicked back to the action on screen. 'Oi, ref! Offside, man!'

I stared at the TV, baffled. 'What does that even mean?'

'What is it with girls and the offside rule? It's simple!'

Crunching defensively on a handful of crisps, I folded my arms. 'Go on, then, David Beckham. Explain.'

A determined gleam in his eye, Dontay sat up straight and scanned the snacks on the coffee table thoughtfully. 'All right. We're going to need salt and pepper pots, one of those cheesy footballs and that glass.'

I gathered everything up and sat back down. What followed confused me more than I'd thought possible. Most ghosts learned how to move solid things around, but it wasn't a skill Dontay had mastered yet. So, with him barking instructions at me, I put the glass in goal and placed the other things in various positions around the table, trying hard to look like I understood every word. As far as I could tell, as long as your pepper pot didn't play the cheesy ball past the salt, you were OK. How that related to what was happening in the actual game was anyone's guess, but Dontay looked so pleased with himself I didn't dare ask anything else.

By the time the teams went off at half-time, England were cruising at two-nil up and the opposition looked like they wished the game was over. Flicking a sideways glance at Dontay, I said, 'I bet you miss it, being able to kick a ball about.'

His expression was bleak. 'It sucks.'

Something had been nagging at me. 'How did you work out how to leave the place you died and move around? Did another ghost tell you?'

'What are you on about?' he asked. 'I didn't need to be told – I just went.'

I frowned. 'It's not as simple as that. Ghosts need to carry something from the place where they died to be able to leave. If you don't, you're stuck there.'

Dontay stuck a hand in his pocket. 'I had this on me when I got shot,' he said, revealing a silver number six the size of his palm. 'It fell off the front door when I slammed it to go and meet my mate. Someone would have nicked it if I left it on the floor so I shoved in my pocket.'

That explained it; Dontay had died on his own doorstep, at the bottom of the tower block. He hadn't needed to take anything because he'd already got the number. 'You're lucky. Some ghosts never figure out how to leave.'

He nodded, turning the number over in his fingers. 'I

didn't go far at first, mostly just up to the flat, but I hated seeing Mum crying all the time. So I started following Nelson when he went training with the lads. In the end, I couldn't stand not being able to join in.' His hand clenched around the metal. 'The ghost of an old bloke in the flat next door told me about the Dearly D, and I knew I had to go.'

'Oh?' I hardly dared to breathe.

'For Nelson. He couldn't cope when I died. I'd always been there for him, see? He looked up to me and suddenly, I was gone.' His voice cracked on the last word. A shuttered look came into his eyes and he swallowed. 'I don't know if I can do this.'

I watched him in mute sympathy. His pain was obvious, but forcing him to face up to it before he was ready wasn't going to help anyone. There was no rush, anyway. At least he'd opened up a bit and I felt he was beginning to trust me. It was enough for now. I decided to lighten the mood.

'If you're planning to put together a ghostly five-a-side team, don't pick Gawjus George,' I advised, pulling a rueful face. 'When he says he's a world-class dribbler, he doesn't mean with a ball.'

He heaved in a deep breath and smiled in spite of himself. 'Cheers, I'll remember that.'

The players reappeared on the screen and we turned our attention to the match. The opposition had clearly been given a real telling-off at half-time because they played like their lives depended on it and it was soon two-all. Dontay divided his time between cheering the England boys on and answering my questions. To be honest, I was feeling pretty pleased with myself. Dontay was relaxing around me and I'd learned that cheesy balls were more important than I'd realised in football; overall, the evening had been a success. But I'd forgotten about one tiny detail, the number one reason why Celestine never, ever invited ghosts back to the house: Mary. As her quivering, enraged form materialised in the doorway, I knew I'd made a huge mistake.

'This place is mine!' she howled, her face twisted in territorial fury. 'Begone, before I unleash the seven spirits of hell on thee!'

Chapter 7

Dontay jumped up, his expression a mixture of bravado and confusion. 'You what?'

I stood too. I didn't know which seven spirits of hell she had in mind, but she was in danger of freaking Dontay out and I didn't want him to run again. Forcing my racing pulse to calm down, I injected a casual tone into my words. 'Relax, Mary, he's visiting, not moving in.' Turning to Dontay, I lowered my voice. 'Don't make any sudden moves, OK?'

She glided closer, mistrust etched on her face. 'Does thy aunt know thou art breaking the covenant?'

Dontay glanced at me helplessly. 'What's she on about? Who is she?'

I rolled my eyes. She was talking about the haunting-rights pact she'd negotiated back in my grandparents' day to ensure no other ghosts muscled in on her personal haunt-fest. Celestine had mentioned it when I'd first moved in, but needless to say, I'd forgotten. 'It's hardly breaking the covenant. This is a friend and we're just watching the game.' I looked from her deeply suspicious face to Dontay's bewildered one and sighed. 'Look, how about if I introduce you? Mary Drover, this is Dontay Ambrose.'

Her wary gaze still trained on Dontay, she waved a hand at the plasma screen. 'What mischief art thou hatching with the sorcerer's tool?'

I shook my head in embarrassed disbelief. Anyone would think she'd only just materialised from the sixteenth century. The truth was she loved the TV as much as I did and I suspected she was a shopping channel addict during the day. I adopted my most persuasive voice. 'Absolutely no mischief has been hatched, Mary. I promise. Celestine knows all about it.'

For a moment, she seemed to teeter on the brink of a major tantrum, but her gaze flickered back to the television screen and I could see she was curious. I signalled Dontay to sit down and sank on to the sofa myself, patting the cushions next to me invitingly. 'Why don't you join us?'

''Tis an unnatural thing,' she muttered, but I could tell her heart wasn't in it. With one last glower at Dontay, she came and sat down. And that was how

Celestine found us twenty minutes later; two teenagers and a four-hundred-year-old witch in deep conversation about the merits of playing a four-four-two formation. From the look of astonishment on her face, it was the unlikeliest sight she'd ever seen.

'Hi.' I grinned up at her. I was about to explain what had happened but England chose that moment to drive the ball into the back of the net to score the winning goal. All three of us leaped off the sofa, cheering, and I didn't care what my ancestors thought.

Celestine watched in puzzled amusement. 'No need to ask how things are going, then,' she said, as Dontay and Mary high-fived. 'Good to meet you at last, Dontay.'

He flashed a shy grin and nodded. I beamed, proud of him and of myself. My goal had been to get him to open up. If things carried on the way they had been going, it looked like England weren't the only ones to have hit the target.

Megan was practically bouncing off the corridor walls when I joined her outside our form room the next morning. Dr Bailey frowned at her as he prowled by, his handlebar moustache quivering with disapproval, but thankfully he didn't speak.

'Have you heard what's happening this afternoon?' she said, almost squeaking with suppressed excitement.

I studied her gleaming eyes and stupidly bouncy grin. 'School is closing early?' I hazarded.

She shook her head. 'Nope.'

I pursed my lips thoughtfully. 'Zombie Bride are doing a secret gig in the dance studio?'

They were Megan's favourite band and I knew she'd give up Oreo cookies for a month to see them play. Her gaze became distant as she got momentarily side-tracked. 'No,' she conceded, 'but that would be monumentally cool. Guess again.'

'Charlie asked you out?'

'Yeah, because *that's* going to happen.' She jiggled impatiently. 'Come on, you're not trying hard enough. What's the most exciting thing you can imagine, like, ever?'

'Why don't you just tell me?' I suggested, raising my eyebrows. 'Before you make a puddle on the floor.'

She leaned in closer. 'The first inter-school sports tournament of the year is next month, so Mrs Robertson has decided that all the Year Tens have to try out for the athletics squad.' She paused to look at me meaningfully. 'This afternoon.'

My heart sank to the bottom of my black pumps. There were few lessons I truly hated but PE was one of them. Quite why Megan was expecting me to get in a lather about it was anyone's guess. 'And?'

She turned her gaze towards the ceiling. 'It means

that both halves of the year will be together. Who do we know in the other half of the year?'

Suddenly, I understood. She meant Nico. 'Megan —'

She clasped her hands together, grinning like a less hairy chimpanzee. 'They all got notes telling them to bring their kit yesterday. It's so perfect! Imagine if he was one of the team captains. I bet he'd pick you first.'

I stared at her helplessly. Where did this idea come from that Nico and me were some kind of star-crossed lovers? I'd hardly mentioned him, and suddenly we were the Bella and Edward of North London. 'He'd wish he hadn't picked me, let me tell you,' I said, my voice grim. 'There's only one thing I'm worse at than sport and that's French.'

'He won't mind. Anyway, you're exaggerating.'

I rolled my eyes. She might be fast becoming my best friend, but she was nuttier than a Snickers bar sometimes. 'You saw me playing hockey last week. How many times did I trip over my own stick?'

Shrugging, she said, 'So hockey isn't your thing. It doesn't matter, anyway. Nico is going to be all over you.'

My treacherous brain conjured up his image and whispered that it wouldn't mind that at all. Out of the corner of my eye I saw Ellie leaning towards us, her eyes narrowed. I pushed the thought firmly out of my head and nudged Megan. 'Shh!'

She folded her arms, smirking. 'Someone's going to

have their nose put right out of joint. I can't wait.'

Glumly, I trailed into the room after Megan. I wouldn't be surprised if she'd planned an outfit for my wedding and named our first kids. How disappointed was she going to be when Nico completely blanked me later?

Despite my best efforts to ignore them, Megan's words nagged at me throughout the morning, not helped by the tiny corner of my brain hoping she was right about Nico. By the time lunch rolled around, I was feeling sick with anxiety. If there'd been a Mr Men character called *Little Miss Clumsy*, I'd have been the model. I wasn't remotely interested in some stupid inter-school competition and Mrs Robertson would be even less keen on having me in her elite squad. It was a form of legalised torture, with the added stress of knowing Nico would be watching. In spite of my vow not to get involved with him, part of me already was.

Megan was beaming at me from the other side of the changing room, but I didn't share her enthusiasm. In fact, I was seriously considering inventing a mystery ailment to get out of the trials altogether. It wouldn't be stretching the truth too much to say I had stomach cramps. But some teachers have in-built lie detectors and Mrs Robertson was one of them. Nothing short of a broken limb would save me, and I wasn't that desperate. Miserably, I pulled my kit on and tried to ignore the daggers Ellie and her mates were firing my way.

Megan started scanning the sports field as soon as we got out there, and it didn't take her long to spot Nico in the crowd.

'There he is!'

I followed her outstretched finger to where Nico stood, his jet-black head clearly visible above those of his friends.

'Oh my God, he's watching you!' she squealed.

Sure enough, Nico was looking our way. Horribly aware that Megan was still pointing at him and feeling my face turn Barbie pink, I snatched her arm down. 'Shut up!'

'But he was,' she insisted, shaking my hand off. 'I told you he fancies you.'

I wasn't denying he'd been looking, but he wasn't any more. Now he was laughing with his mates and there were no prizes for guessing what the joke was. Maybe he was telling them what a freak I was.

'Just leave it, Megan,' I mumbled, turning my back on Nico and willing my rosy cheeks to cool down. I obviously wasn't cut out to be the heroine of a doomed romance – they never blushed.

Mrs Robertson trotted over in her trademark polyester tracksuit. 'Come along, girls, get a move on.' She stopped and surveyed us critically. 'Megan, you did well at high jump last year. Why don't you work on that again?'

Her gaze travelled down to the top of my head, which was somewhere around the level of Megan's earlobe. 'Hmm, what are we going to do with you?'

Please let her take pity on me and send me back to the changing rooms, I prayed, trying to look as useless at sport as possible. Typically, my efforts were wasted. 'How do you fancy a go at the triple jump?'

My mouth fell open. Triple jump? Didn't you need the speed of a cheetah and the legs of a supermodel to do that properly? She had to be joking.

I looked up at her glowing-with-health face for a twinkly-eyed smile. There wasn't one.

'You don't think I'm a bit, um, short for that, miss?'

'Nonsense,' she said, shaking her head. She glanced around as though searching for someone. 'Ellie, show Skye here the basics of the triple jump.'

I groaned silently. As if the afternoon wasn't bad enough, I was about to be introduced to the ways of the hop, skip and jump by someone who wouldn't mind at all if I broke my neck in the sandpit. Perfect.

Ellie sauntered up and smirked at me. 'Of course, Mrs Robertson.'

'Great.' Mrs Robertson patted her on the shoulder, then turned to Megan. 'You can come with me. The high jump is over the other side of the field.'

Pulling a sympathetic face, Megan followed her across the field, leaving me with Ellie.

'Ready?' she said, wearing what looked like a genuine smile.

I blinked. Had I got the wrong idea about her? Maybe she wasn't a total cow after all. 'As ready as I'll ever be.'

Her smile hardened. 'Good. Because I'm about to make you wish your little Scottish arse had never been born.'

Crap. Obviously I hadn't got the wrong idea after all.

Chapter 8

If you've ever been to Oxford Circus in London, you've probably had an earful from the preachers who hang around there. You know the type I mean; all brimstone and hellfire, warning you to repent your sins or face an eternity of suffering. If they'd told me hell was an endless afternoon of triple-jump failure, with thirty or so other kids as witness to your utter humiliation, I'd have abandoned my sinful ways immediately. The only blessing was that Nico hadn't seen. Knowing he was watching me put the 'trip' in triple jump would have just about finished me off.

Ellie didn't mess about in making me wish I'd never been born. She took malicious delight in every stumble, and on the rare occasion when I didn't fall over my own feet, she declared the jump void. It didn't help that the other triple jumpers had the grace of gazelles and managed very respectable jumps. Needless to say, Ellie was one of them. With her dark hair streaming out behind her as she soared over the sandpit, she looked like a Greek goddess. Either that or a giant bat, I decided sourly as she scored another four-metre jump. It felt as though the lesson was never going to end.

'How's it going?' Mrs Robertson's gaze was bright and expectant as she jogged towards us. 'Any budding district champions?'

Ellie smiled. 'A few possibilities, miss.'

Mrs Robertson looked at me. 'How about you, Skye? Did you manage to find your rhythm?'

Ellie snorted with laughter and quickly turned it into a cough. 'Not exactly.'

Most of the groups had finished their trials and the other kids were drifting over to where we stood. Ellie raised her voice. 'I don't think she's got what it takes.'

Even Mrs Robertson couldn't miss her scornful tone. 'Really, Ellie? I think I'll be the judge of that.' She turned to me and smiled. 'Show us what you're made of, Skye.'

I stared at her, doing my best paralysed rabbit impression. So she wanted to know what I was made of, did she? Judging from this afternoon's evidence, it was mostly left feet. Mrs Robertson gave me a nod of encouragement and over her shoulder I could see

Megan waving crossed fingers at me. With a glum sigh, I dragged myself to the start of the run-up. I could practically feel Ellie willing me to cock it up.

Then the weirdest thing happened. As I stared along the path to the jump line and the sandpit beyond, all of the frustration of the afternoon suddenly bubbled up inside me. Why was I letting Ellie make me feel bad about myself? I'd done a couple of reasonable jumps already, hadn't I? There was no reason why I couldn't do another one now.

Holding on tight to this unexpected determination, I steamed along the path and concentrated on hitting the board exactly right. With a powerful bound, I hopped with my right foot, skipped with my left – and then I made a fatal mistake: my eyes strayed sideways into the crowd. Standing beside the sandpit was Nico, watching me intently. Distracted by his dark stare, I forgot to check the position of my leading foot before launching into my jump. There was a confused jumble of floor and trainers – it felt like I had at least three feet at one point – before I lost my balance and my ankle twisted underneath me. The next thing I knew, I lurched through the air and crumpled into an undignified heap in the sand.

'Less than a metre,' I heard Ellie say in a self-satisfied manner. 'I did say she wasn't very good.'

Mrs Robertson's expression was a mixture of anger and disgust. 'She'd have been a lot better if you hadn't stuck your foot out, Ellie McCauley. Don't think I didn't see you.'

Ellie went pale. 'I don't know what happened, miss. I think I sort of slipped.'

Lips pursed, Mrs Robertson looked like she didn't buy a word of it. 'There's no room for cheats on my team, Ellie. Go back to the changing room and get dressed. I'll deal with you later.'

For a second, I thought Ellie was going to argue, but instead she burst into tears and ran from the field. Fierce whispers broke out around us.

I cleared my throat. 'Could I get a little help here?'

Megan gave a guilty gasp and pushed forwards to help me up, but she was beaten to it. Nico reached down and offered me his hand. 'Are you OK?'

I rubbed the sand away from my lips, but left the grains on my cheeks. Maybe they'd help to mask the fierce blush crawling up my face. I always seemed to be going red when he was around. Was I allergic to him or something?

Mrs Robertson bustled over. 'Anything broken?'

I shook my head. 'No, I'm fine.'

Realising Nico was still waiting to help me up, I reached up shyly and took his hand, half expecting a jolt of electricity to hit me as we touched. It didn't; his fingers were cool on mine and his grip was strong as he drew me upwards. Our eyes locked and the rest of the kids faded into the background. Maybe Megan was right, I thought dreamily as I drank in his gaze. Maybe we were a pair of star-crossed —

'Ow!' A knife-like pain snaked up my leg and killed the moment stone dead.

'What's wrong?' Mrs Robertson asked, her face concerned.

I grimaced and slid a hand down my calf. 'My ankle hurts. I think I twisted it.'

'I can't really leave the class unattended.' She glanced around and her eyes settled on Nico. 'Could you take her to the nurse, please, Nico?'

Megan stepped forward. 'I'll go too.'

'Oh no,' Mrs Robertson said. 'You're staying right here to practise that high jump. A few more attempts and you'll have smashed your personal best. Nico can take care of Skye.'

The words sent a delicious shiver along my spine, in spite of what felt like a thousand pointy-toothed goblins chewing on my ankle. I liked the idea of Nico taking care of me. Megan appeared to be torn between wanting to know whether she was right about Nico and delight at Mrs Robertson's praise. She made a texting gesture with her thumbs.

'OK,' I agreed and, leaning awkwardly on Nico's arm, I limped off the field towards the office.

Neither of us spoke until we were away from the crowd.

'Thanks,' I said, as much to break the silence as anything.

'No problem.' He concentrated on supporting me for a few more steps before continuing, 'We seem to keep bumping into each other. I'm Nico Albescu.'

I threw a sideways glance at him. Up close, he seemed taller, which made me feel even more Tinkerbell-esque than usual. The contrast between his pale skin and black hair was more pronounced too; I could see long sooty lashes framing his dark eyes. My gaze slid to his hair, lying carelessly against the collar of his PE shirt. Was it too long because he liked it that way or because he didn't care about his looks? 'Skye Thackery.'

We limped along without speaking for several seconds. Even through the burning throb of my ankle I was aware of his body pressed against mine. I couldn't tell if it was the pain from my ankle or Nico's closeness, but my heart was racing so much I felt sure he must be able to hear it thudding. Distractedly, I said, 'Sorry about this.'

'Don't be. To be honest, I wanted an excuse to introduce myself all week. I nearly did it at lunch today, but you were with your friend and I didn't want to interrupt.'

The pain was rudely shoved out of the way by the sharp twist of my guts as realisation sank in. I had sat with Megan at lunchtime. So she'd been bang on the money; he had been looking out for me. Which could only mean —

'So what have you done to annoy Ellie?' he asked, oblivious to my stuttering heart rate.

Just how was I supposed to answer that, given that he was the main reason Ellie hated me? 'Dunno. I think she's a bit unstable.'

He threw me an odd look. 'I'd have thought you'd have been a bit more understanding.'

It took me a minute to work out what he meant. I replayed the words inside my head and cringed. For a girl with a supposed mental illness I didn't sound in the least bit sympathetic. 'Oh. Erm – well, Ellie's nothing like me, she's plain nasty, whereas I'm just —'

'A bit weird?' he finished, smiling.

I had no defence. 'Yeah, I suppose so.'

'Don't worry, weird is good. It makes you stand out from the crowd.'

It was easy for him to say; he didn't know how different I really was. But I preferred to think that he'd noticed me in spite of my off-the-wall behaviour, so I decided to change the subject. 'I think my career as a triple jumper may be over.'

He grinned and held open the door to the main reception for me to half hop, half limp through. It was the first time I'd seen him smile and it changed his features from intense and brooding to gob-stoppingly handsome. I'd never understood what the word 'swoon' meant before; I did now.

'Oh, I don't know,' he said. 'You could be the one everyone underestimates.'

I nodded, picturing the scene at the regional competition. 'Then I start my run-up and it's hop, skip, jump and finish with a spectacular face plant in the sand.'

We looked at each other and burst out laughing.

'I was rubbish, wasn't I?'

Nico's laughter slowed. 'Yeah, but I bet you've got other talents, right?'

I think that was the exact moment that I gave up fighting the attraction, although to be fair, it hadn't been much of a fight. He was gorgeous. He was interested. I'd have to be dead not to want to snog him, and I definitely wasn't dead. 'I do, as it happens.'

It was his move. I waited, not daring to breathe. His lips parted. If this was a rom-com, he'd be about to ask me out.

'Skye!' a voice bellowed. My head jerked up and I stared wildly around the hallway. Dontay was watching us through heavily lidded eyes. And he did not look happy.

Chapter 9

I did what any sensible person would have done. I froze.

Nico stopped. 'What's the matter? Are you OK?'

Unsticking my tongue from the roof of my mouth, I forced my lips to work.

'I'm fine,' I mumbled. What the hell was Dontay doing here? How did he even know which school I went to?

Frowning, Nico said, 'You're shaking.'

I was. In fact, I felt like I was about to have an out-of-body experience at any second. I could hardly back out of seeing the nurse without making Nico suspicious, but I couldn't talk to Dontay either. When he came over, I'd be forced to do something I'd never done before. In all my fourteen years, I'd never ignored a ghost. He'd understand, wouldn't he?

'Delayed shock, I suppose,' I said, dredging up a smile. 'I'll be OK in a minute.'

There was nothing for it; I was going to have to face the music. With my eyes fixed straight ahead and my teeth firmly gritted, I leaned on Nico and limped towards the double doors.

Dontay waited until we were through the doors and level with him before he spoke. He eyed my crumpled state impassively and got straight to the point. 'What's going on?'

Pressing my lips together, I threw him an imploring look and concentrated on reaching the nurse.

Dontay's expression darkened. 'Who's this? You never said you had a boyfriend.'

He sounded like he was accusing me of something, but I couldn't work out what. Every one of my brain cells was screaming at me to reply. No one else even knew he was there, but for me he was as real as the living, and ignoring him went against everything I valued. I could see the anger building inside him and squeezed my eyes closed, relying on Nico to lead me the last few metres. Surely Dontay knew I couldn't answer?

'Can I ask you something?' Nico said.

Dontay stepped in front of me. 'Don't ignore me.'

That was it. My resolve snapped. 'Not now, OK?'

Dontay shrugged and backed off. 'Whatever.'

He turned and slouched through the double doors. I

knew he was hurt, but I couldn't do anything to make it better.

Beside me, Nico was staring at me in confusion. 'Right. Sorry.'

Crap. I'd forgotten Nico had asked me a question. He'd obviously thought I was answering him. I gave myself a mental slap – of course he had, who else was there? 'No, I'm sorry. My ankle is making me a bit crabby.'

'Does it really hurt?' he asked.

Actually it was starting to ease off, but I couldn't very well tell him that now. 'Yeah.' I glanced up to see that we'd made it to the door of the nurse's office. 'Thanks for the, er, lift.'

'No problem.' He hesitated and studied me for a few seconds. 'Listen, I've got a spare ticket for The Droids gig at the Roundhouse in Camden next Saturday. I was going to ask if you wanted to come. If your ankle is better, that is.'

I swallowed hard and resisted the temptation to pinch myself. Had I heard him right? In spite of the fact that I was as graceful as an elephant on roller skates, and in spite of hearing me talking to myself on two separate occasions, Nico was asking me out. I couldn't believe it; Nico was asking *me* out! And we were going to see one of my favourite bands ever, on a date, like normal people. My heart tapped out a happy little dance. And then I caught a glimpse of Dontay through the glass door and reality came crashing in. My life was about as far away from normal as it was possible to get. Could I risk getting close to Nico? How would he react if he learned how deep the weirdness went?

I reached down and massaged my leg to buy myself time. 'Saturday?'

He nodded. To anyone watching, Nico looked relaxed, but his stillness told me he was anything but as he waited for me to answer. Every part of me wanted to say yes – every part except my brain. 'I can't,' I said. 'Sorry.'

A flash of disappointment crossed his face and he glanced away. 'No problem. I've got a mate who'll take the ticket.'

My throat closed in misery. I couldn't believe I'd just turned down a date with the hottest boy in school. I swallowed. 'Have a good time.'

He looked at me and I wondered if he was going to ask me why I'd said no. But he must have seen something in my face, or maybe he had too much pride. Whatever the reason, he glanced instead at the nurse's office door. 'Will you be all right on your own?'

Somehow, I managed to tilt my head yes. I didn't dare try to speak; tears were too close.

He smiled briefly. 'See you around, then.'

Watching him cross the hall, I willed him to glance

back. If he did, it meant he was still interested. When the double doors swung shut after him, I knew I'd lost my chance, and the fact that I'd done the right thing was no consolation. Dontay fired an ungrateful scowl in my direction, then turned away. I raised my hand to rap on the wooden door and choked down a silent sob. It was the first time I'd had to choose the dead over the living. I hoped it would be the last.

'Whose idea was this again?'

I rubbed my icy fingers together and glared first at Jeremy and then at Dontay. It was the next day, Saturday, and for reasons which had seemed perfectly sane in the comfort of Celestine's living room the night before, we were freezing our noses off on the touchline of one of the football pitches at Hackney Marshes, watching Dontay's brother play. Although Dontay had got over his tantrum at the school and understood why I'd ignored him, I still felt like I needed to make it up to him. After my initial misery had faded, I found I couldn't blame him for what had happened with Nico. I'd always known being psychic meant I'd have to be careful who I got close to. Besides, Dontay wasn't exactly overwhelmed with things to do during the day; I'd be crawling the walls with boredom if I was him, so I'd agreed to hang out with him more and going along to the football was part of the deal. There were teams playing as far as the eye could see and it felt like half the teenage boys in London were there with us. Girls were in short supply; I reckoned I was outnumbered by about fifty to one. And I was grateful Jeremy had decided to come along. To the casual observer it looked like I was talking to him. And he'd brought a flask of hot Ribena.

'Shut up moaning, yeah?' Dontay said absently as he watched Nelson weave past a defender and head towards the goal. 'It's not even cold.'

I clasped my arms around myself and jiggled up and down on the spot, wincing every now and then from the twinges in my strapped-up ankle. 'That's easy for you to say. Ghosts don't feel temperature. It could be sub-zero and you wouldn't know it.'

'I told you to wear a hat and gloves,' Jeremy pointed out in a mildly self-satisfied voice. 'I did say it would be chilly.'

I didn't even dignify that with an answer and turned to Dontay instead. 'So this is where you used to play?'

He nodded. 'Until I got picked up by the Hammers. Then I played at their training ground in Essex with the other Academy kids.' He trailed off as the goalkeeper saved a shot aimed at the back of the net. 'I'd give anything to kick the ball about again.'

The longing in his voice was almost tangible. A wave of sympathy crashed over me and we watched in silence as the game went on in front of us. In spite of what I'd learned watching the England game with Dontay, I still felt like I knew nothing about football, but even I could see Nelson was a talented player. The ball seemed tied to his feet with invisible string as he danced around the opposing team. If Dontay had been anything like as good as his brother then he'd been robbed of a shining future. No wonder he was bitter and angry.

I still hadn't spoken to him about his death. If I was honest, I still wasn't sure how to broach the subject without upsetting him. He was starting to open up, but he was often still moody and I didn't feel we were at the stage where I could force him to relive painful memories. I couldn't help feeling it was somehow linked to Nelson, though, which was why I'd agreed to give up my precious Saturday morning lie-in for gloomy Hackney.

There was nothing useful I could say to Dontay, so I clamped my mouth closed and we watched the game. He sank into a brooding silence and I could practically feel his barely contained resentment seething beside me. It wasn't until his brother threaded the ball past the keeper and we were watching the players jog back to the halfway line that Dontay seemed to shake himself out of his mood and I decided to take a risk.

'Can I ask you something?'

He shrugged, throwing me a curious look. 'I suppose so, yeah.'

'What do you miss most about being alive?' Jeremy

threw me a warning glance, but I ignored him and waved a hand towards the pitch. 'Apart from this, obviously.'

Dontay thrust his hands into his pockets, staring down at the patchy white touchline peeping through the muddy grass at our feet. 'Loads of stuff,' he said, his voice subdued. 'My mates, my family. Krispy Kreme doughnuts.' His eyes met mine and behind the resentment, I saw misery etched there. 'Everything, really.'

I swallowed my sympathy and forced myself to push on. 'Why do you think you're still here?'

His gaze flickered briefly towards the pitch. 'Dunno. Maybe you can figure that out.'

I opened my mouth to reply, but a crunching tackle right in front of us had me leaping backwards to avoid a jumble of legs. By the time the referee had waved the yellow card at one of the players, Dontay had moved away from me and it was clear he wasn't in a talking mood.

'How's things?' Jeremy handed me a steaming cup of blackcurrant juiciness and eyed me meaningfully. 'Everything OK?'

I guessed he meant how were things going with Dontay. I cast an uneasy glance towards him, not sure he was far enough away for me to give Jeremy an honest answer. But his attention was fixed on the game. Now that I came to think of it, it had to be a bit weird for Jeremy, knowing that there were ghosts nearby but not being able to see or hear them. No wonder he got the wrong end of the stick so often when he heard Celestine or me bickering with Mary.

'Not great,' I replied. 'All things being equal, I'd rather be in bed. And it was a bit weird having him turn up at school yesterday. He didn't seem to get why I couldn't talk to him.'

'Believe me, I know that feeling,' Jeremy said in a heartfelt voice. 'Lucy got me into all kinds of sticky situations when other people were around. I'm amazed I wasn't locked up, actually.'

Something else was bothering me. 'The way he spoke, it sounded like he almost resented me.'

'He probably does, a bit. Think about it, you have everything he doesn't.'

Not everything, I thought, as an image of Nico flashed into my mind. I could see what Jeremy was getting at, and Dontay's attitude kind of made sense, but my life was a long way from perfect. 'What, like double maths first thing on a Monday morning, you mean?'

'Cut him some slack,' Jeremy advised. 'From what you and Celestine have said, he seems like a good kid.'

Annoyingly, he was right. 'That's why I can't feel my toes right now.'

Jeremy nodded in sympathy. 'Look on the bright side. You might be watching a future Premiership footballer among this lot.'

I pulled a face and watched in thoughtful silence as Nelson made another dart forwards. Maybe Jeremy wasn't talking complete rubbish; Dontay might not know for sure why he hadn't passed across, but I was willing to bet my glittery eyeliner it had something to do with his younger brother. Who was to say that Dontay wasn't destined to help Nelson make something of his life? One thing I did know: if I had any hope at all of helping Dontay, I had to find a way to fully earn his trust and that wouldn't happen if he still resented me. As the referee blew his whistle and Nelson's team gave each other congratulatory thumps on the arm, an idea popped into my head. Should I run it past Dontay first? I decided not to; he'd only try to stop me.

'Wait here,' I told Jeremy, passing him my half-drunk cup of Ribena and hobbling on to the pitch.

Dontay's narrowed gaze drilled into my back as I approached Nelson. I squared my shoulders and ignored him.

'Hi,' I called as soon as I was near enough. 'Great goal.'

Nelson stopped mid calf stretch to look up. 'Thanks.'

Taking a deep breath, I ploughed on. 'You're Nelson Ambrose, right?'

Frowning, he straightened slowly. 'Yeah. Do I know you?'

OK, this was it, I told myself. Don't freak him out. 'Not exactly, but I know your brother.'

He stared at me and I realised what I'd said.

'Knew,' I amended hastily, aware that Dontay had followed me on to the pitch and was listening to every word. 'I meant I knew him. Before, you know . . .'

Nelson watched me, his forehead creased into a suspicious frown. 'What's your name?'

'Skye Thackery,' I replied, my palms starting to sweat as I realised I hadn't thought this through.

His frown deepened. 'He never mentioned you. Where d'you know him from?'

I froze. I had approximately three seconds to come up with a likely location where I might have met Dontay, and my brain had gone completely blank. I could hardly say the Church of the Dearly Departed, could I?

'Tell him we met at the snooker hall down Homerton High Street.' Dontay sounded like he was trying not to laugh as he took pity on me. 'It's over-sixteens only so Mum never let him go there.'

I jumped on the words gratefully. 'We played snooker.'

Nelson looked me up and down in disbelief. 'No offence, but you don't look old enough. Or tall enough to reach the table.'

'I'm sixteen,' I lied. 'And if you must know, I stood on a box.'

Dontay and Nelson snorted at exactly the same moment, their laughter ringing across the chilly field in stereo.

'He would have told me about something like that,' Nelson said, his amusement subsiding. 'Who sent you? Are you one of the Marsh Street Massive? Cos if you are —'

'No!' I cut in, stung. 'I don't even know who they are. I just knew Dontay, that's all.' My gaze flickered over my shoulder. 'We were mates.'

Nelson's expression was still distrustful. 'Yeah, well can't be too careful. Shank said they'd be trying to get to me and it'd be just like the Marsh Street arseholes to send a girl to stitch me up.'

I didn't have the faintest idea what he was going on about or who Shank was, but it wasn't the right time to ask. Clenching my hands into fists by my side, I pushed on. 'You must miss him. Dontay, I mean.'

Instantly, his expression became shuttered and he stared at his feet. 'Of course I do. He was my brother.'

'Nelson!' A middle-aged man in a crimson tracksuit bellowed and waved an arm. 'Stop chatting up the birds and get over here for cool-down.'

Nelson glanced around and I thought I caught a hint of relief on his dark face. 'I have to go. See ya.'

He jogged towards the rest of the team and didn't look back. Seeing him go, Jeremy headed my way.

'See you around,' I called after Nelson, not sure if I'd actually achieved anything. It wasn't until I turned to look at Dontay that I got my answer. His eyes glittered with something indefinable as he watched his brother.

'He seems like a good kid,' I offered. 'Who are the Marsh Street Massive? And who's Skank?'

Jeremy's eyebrows shot up. 'Skank? Isn't that an illegal substance?'

My jaw dropped. Who'd have thought Jeremy was so well up on his drug-related slang?

'Keep it down,' Dontay muttered, glancing around to see if any of the footballers had heard. When he saw no one was listening, he went on. 'It's Shank, not Skank. He's the main man in the London Fields Posse and he's like a god in Hackney. If anyone hears you so much as breathing wrong around him, you'll end up like me.'

'That's your gang, right?' I said tentatively, recalling our first ever conversation outside the Dearly D.'

The same strange look as last time crossed his face; half proud, half disdainful. 'Sort of. I wasn't really a proper member, just sort of hung around with them. The Marsh Street Massive is a rival gang, not as big but twice as vicious.' He focused on his brother stretching some distance away, and his voice tightened with anger. 'I warned Nelson not to get involved with any of them.

He's destined for better things than petty fights over stupid crap.'

In a flash, I knew why Dontay was still here. His brother was getting sucked into gang culture and it was his job to stop it happening. From the look on his face, he knew it too. The question was, what could I do to help? I blew on my chilled fingers ruefully. More importantly, how many Saturday morning lie-ins would it cost me to do it?

Chapter 10

My ankle was much better by Monday, but that didn't stop me accepting Jeremy's offer of a lift to school. His car might have less street-cred than Noddy's, but it did have a wicked sound system and I amused myself on the journey by channel hopping between radio stations in search of a thumping bass-line.

Jeremy frowned in disapproval. 'Pick a station and stick with it,' he said, watching me stab one little button after another. 'What's wrong with Radio Two?'

'Nothing, if you're eighty,' I responded, pausing to listen to a few bars of music before pressing the buttons once more. 'Why do you have such an awesome sound system if all you listen to is Radio Oldster?'

'Just because it plays the classics instead of head-banging mash-downs doesn't make it worthless,' Jeremy argued. 'Have you even heard of Pink Floyd?'

I had a vague idea he was a celebrity chef, but at that moment I found a tune I'd been longing to hear and sat back to enjoy it, my eyes shut so I couldn't see the look of pained incomprehension on Jeremy's face. So I didn't notice we'd reached Hornsey Lane Bridge until Jeremy slammed on the brakes. My eyes flew open as I jerked forwards in my seat.

'What is it?' I gasped, expecting to see a startled pedestrian in the road ahead of us. Instead, I saw the receding bumper of the car in front.

Jeremy's face was white. 'I saw a woman on the bridge.'

My gaze skittered towards the pavement. There were plenty of people crossing the bridge and some of them were women. It didn't explain why Jeremy had stopped. Then I realised what he meant and my eyes narrowed. 'On the bridge? Or jumping off it?'

He passed a shaking hand over his features. 'She jumped, just like you said.'

We stared at the parapet of the bridge; there was no sign that anything out of the ordinary had happened. The sudden blare of a car horn made us both jump. Jeremy shook himself and turned to face the front. Fumbling with the gear stick, he eased the car forwards. Neither of us spoke for a minute, then I said, 'What just happened? You don't see ghosts.'

Jeremy looked as confused as I felt. 'Apart from Lucy, you mean? That definitely wasn't her.'

I battled not to roll my eyes. Lucy had passed across; she wasn't going to be throwing herself off a bridge in North London, unless the astral plane really sucked.

'You're sure the woman jumped?' I asked, but even as the words left my mouth I knew it was a stupid question. Jeremy was part psychic, and what were the chances of making a mistake like that in the exact same spot I'd seen someone jump the week before?

He peered in the rear-view mirror at the bridge behind us. 'I think so. One minute she was there, balancing on the edge, and the next minute she'd disappeared. Where else could she have gone?'

Questions jostled for my attention. How psychic was Jeremy? And why could he see this ghost, but not Mary? I thought back over what he'd told me about Lucy. 'Maybe you only see suicides.'

Jeremy shook his head. 'Lucy was murdered. Her friend, Hep, killed herself and I never saw her.'

I glanced out of the window. Murder and suicide were tragic in any circumstances, but when the victims were around my age I found them even harder to contemplate. 'I don't know, then. Celestine might be able to explain.'

He cast a weak smile my way. 'Let's hope so.'

I didn't have the heart to insist he dropped me off where no one could see. As he pulled up outside the school gates, I reached across and gave him an awkward hug. 'Thanks for the lift. Sorry about the, um, scenery.'

Nodding, he said, 'You're welcome.'

Opening the door, I started to get out.

'Skye?' Jeremy said, as I slammed the door.

I ducked my head through the open window, expecting to be told to treat the car with more respect. 'Yeah?'

'We don't see many friends of yours, apart from Dontay.' He hesitated, then carried on. 'Make sure you spend some time with the living ones too. Dontay might not be around forever.'

I nodded. 'OK.'

Standing back, I watched him drive away and then walked thoughtfully into school. I spotted Dr Bailey in the middle of the hordes of students, bellowing ineffectually, and I ducked behind a group of hulking Year Elevens. I wasn't about to bring any of my schoolmates home. As I'd learned the hard way on Friday afternoon, the living and the dead don't mix.

I didn't tell Megan I'd turned Nico down; she'd have only beaten me to a pulp with her statistics book, and it had at least three hundred pages. But by Tuesday morning my reluctance to discuss him was making her suspicious.

'You were touching all the way from the field to the

nurse's office. You must have talked about something,' she insisted as we sat on the boulders by the rock garden.

'Yeah, we did.'

'And?'

I lifted my shoulders. 'And then I saw the nurse.'

She swatted me with her open hand. 'Didn't he ask you out?'

'No,' I said, crossing my fingers in my blazer pocket. 'I don't think he's interested.'

Squinting at me, she looked like she didn't believe me. 'Really?'

'Yep. It's fine. I don't fancy him anyway.'

It was just as well I wasn't related to Pinocchio or my nose would have been ten centimetres long. Megan sniffed. 'So you won't care that he's coming over here right now, then?'

My head jolted up. Sure enough, Nico was crossing the playground towards me.

Megan stood up. 'Tell me everything,' she whispered, before hurrying away.

Nico's shadow fell over me. 'Hi.'

I shaded my eyes with one hand. 'Hello.'

'Can I sit down?'

'Yeah.' I waved at the boulder beside me. 'Although I warn you, they're not the most comfortable seats in the world.'

Nico arranged himself on the rock next to me. I

couldn't help noticing how close his legs were to mine. Memories of Friday afternoon came flooding back, when he'd practically had his arm around me. I concentrated very hard on a ladybird crawling along the floor and didn't look at him.

'How's the ankle?' he asked.

Flexing it gingerly, I said, 'It's OK. Unless Mrs Robertson is asking in which case I'm in agony.'

'I get you.' Nico smiled and my heart bumped against my ribs. 'I didn't mean to freak you out on Friday. Sorry if I came on a bit strong.'

He'd come on exactly the way I'd hoped he would and if Dontay hadn't turned up, I'd have said yes. I lowered my ankle, wishing I could be honest with him. 'You didn't.'

There was a pause, then he said, 'So you don't hate me, then?'

I looked up. He was grinning, but his eyes were studying me. I swallowed, feeling suddenly light-headed; hate was the exact polar opposite of what I felt. 'I definitely don't hate you.'

'Maybe we could go for a drink or something, then?'

I hesitated. He was by far the coolest boy I'd ever met and this was the second time he'd asked me out. If I said no this time, I didn't think he'd ask again. But how could I risk anyone finding out the truth about me? I stared at Nico as he waited for me to answer, caught up in the dilemma. Then Jeremy's words came back to me, reminding me I needed living friends too, and I came to a sudden decision. I couldn't let my psychic ability rule my life; it wouldn't be easy, but I'd find a way to keep my secret safe.

Over Nico's shoulder, I suddenly caught sight of Megan, hiding behind a bush and grinning like a chimpanzee. The moment she saw me looking, she began twisting her hand wildly between thumbs up and thumbs down and looked so ridiculous that I couldn't help smiling.

Blotting Megan out, I focused on Nico. 'Actually, I'm free on Saturday if you've still got the ticket?'

He threw me a pleased but surprised look. 'Really? You're up for the gig?'

'Yeah, I – uh – thought I was busy but I'm not,' I said, trying to sound as casual as I could. 'I love The Droids.'

He nodded, looking pleased. 'I'll check what time it starts and we can arrange where we're going to meet. Or I can pick you up if you like?'

I gulped. Er – how about no? I might be ready to take a few risks, but Celestine's house was a minefield of potential weirdness; there was no way I was letting him see how freakish I really was. Coming across as a little bit kooky was one thing; having him think I was certifiably insane was quite another.

'Let's meet somewhere,' I said and then I realised how far away Saturday actually was. Could I really wait that long? 'But we could go for a drink before then, if you wanted? There's a new juice bar in Highgate Village.'

His face split into a grin. 'Cool. We should swap mobile numbers, then.'

My heart abandoned its happy dance and went all out for a full-on trapeze act. I grinned back at him, then realised he had his phone out and was waiting for my number. Hurriedly, I reeled off the numbers and he pressed the call button. Seconds later, my mobile vibrated in my blazer. I pulled it out and saved his number.

'So I'll meet you after school?' I said, hoping he wasn't the type to be put off by enthusiasm.

His face clouded. 'I can't do tonight. I kind of work for my dad sometimes and he's got a job for me later. How about tomorrow?'

I could wait one more day. 'Yeah, OK.'

When he was completely out of sight I punched the air in Megan's direction. I had a date with the boy every girl in Heath Park wanted to get to know. I was starting to feel I'd done the right thing by moving down from Scotland. It looked like things were finally on the up.

We'd arranged to meet on Saturday outside Chalk Farm tube station. I'd been quite restrained with the text messaging and had resisted the urge to drop him flirty little texts asking what he was doing every half an hour. I hadn't even been tempted by Megan's suggestion to tap his mobile number into a website to track his location by GPS. I wanted to be his girlfriend, not his stalker.

My stomach cartwheeled crazily when I spotted his dark head above the crowd. Even though we'd gone to the juice bar twice after school that week, I still felt nervous around him – but in a good way, like I did when I was a kid waiting for Christmas Day. Trying to ignore the butterflies flapping up a storm inside me, I weaved towards him.

'Hey,' I said as I reached him. He was dressed from head to toe in black. I gulped at how good-looking he was. It was the first time I'd seen him out of school uniform. If I didn't know better, I'd have said he was playing the gig rather than being in the audience, and judging from the admiring glances he was getting, the rest of the female population thought so too.

He broke into a smile. 'You made it.'

I thought I caught a hint of relief around his eyes. Surely he hadn't been worried I'd stand him up? 'Yeah. Did you think I'd change my mind?'

A teasing expression crept over his face. 'It wouldn't have been the first time. How's the ankle?'

'It's fine, as long as you don't drag me into the mosh pit tonight.'

Mouth quirking, he said, 'Moshing is the last thing on my mind, believe me. Want to head in?'

I gave a distracted nod, glad he wouldn't be leaping around like a lunatic but wondering what he did have on his mind. Was he imagining what it would be like to press his lips against mine, the same as me? I shook the idea away as we followed the crowd along the road, in case I accidentally thought out loud. Once the Roundhouse came into view, I could see where it got its name. Rising up against the orange glow of the city sky was a circular building, easily the most distinctive one around.

We joined the queue to get in. Noticing me craning my head backwards to look at it, Nico said, 'It's not the biggest venue around but it's one of the best for atmosphere and acoustics. Anyone who's anyone has played here.'

The passion in his voice caught my attention and I realised I hardly knew anything about him. 'Are you a musician?'

A wry grin tugged at his mouth. 'Nah. I look the part, but the sad truth is that I'm tone deaf. You?'

I waved an airy hand. 'Oh yeah, I'm very musical.'

He threw me an impressed look. 'What do you play?'

Pretending to think, I tapped my lips slowly. 'If I had to narrow it down, I'd say my best instrument is the triangle.'

A snort of laughter escaped him.

'What?' I said, opening my eyes wide in mock hurt. 'It's a very complex instrument. Not just anyone can play it, you know, it takes years of practice.'

Eyes still crinkled with amusement, he looked down at me. 'I'll take your word for it.'

We'd reached the front of the queue. Nico reached into his leather jacket and pulled out two tickets. The security guard inspected them, then studied me.

'You have to be fourteen to come in here without an adult. Got any ID?'

I could have kicked myself. How many times in the past had I been asked to prove I was older than I looked? Too many was the answer, so why hadn't I thought of bringing something along tonight? My shoulders drooped miserably. 'I don't have anything.'

Nico thrust a hand into the back pocket of his jeans and pulled out a shiny rectangle. 'Don't worry, I've got your school library card here. Will that do?'

I stared first at him, then at the laminated card in his hand, utterly confused. I hadn't been given a library card yet. How could Nico have one with my name, date of birth and photo on it?

The man examined the library card closely, before handing it back to Nico. 'You don't look fifteen.' He motioned us inside. 'In you go, then.'

I opened my mouth to tell him I was fourteen and

then closed it again; it would only complicate things. Keeping my eyes firmly away from the guard, in case he somehow read my mind, I followed Nico through the gate and into the foyer. Once we were out of earshot of the security guard, I said, 'Where did you get that card?'

He shrugged. 'I've been coming here for years so I knew they'd ask for ID. I didn't know if you had anything so I made one for you.'

My hand snaked towards him. 'Let me see.'

He passed me the fake card. It looked just like the ones everyone at Heath Park used and had my correct name and a smiling photograph of me. My date of birth was shown as the fifteenth of August but the year was out. 'So that's why he thought I was fifteen,' I said. 'Right date, wrong year. And where did you get that photo?'

'Facebook,' he replied. 'I thought you could use it to get into fifteen certificate films as well.'

I was trying my hardest not to be a little freaked out. On one hand I was touched that he'd thought I might need ID and had gone to the trouble of making sure I could get into the gig. On the other hand, it wasn't exactly normal date behaviour. Why hadn't he just texted me to tell me to bring something? I held the card towards him but he shook his head.

'Keep it for next time,' he said and smiled in a way that flipped my stomach like a pancake. 'Come on, let's head upstairs. The support act will be on in a minute.'

He led the way up to the first floor and through a set of double doors. The moment we stepped through them and into the circular gig arena, I could see why bands would love to play there; it was one of the most intimate venues I'd ever seen. The stage was only a metre or so higher than the crowd and close enough for the musicians to be able to drink in the adoration of their fans. Even though we were close to the back of the room, I could see everything perfectly. As the support act took to the stage, the crowd surged and roared their appreciation. The atmosphere was charged with anticipation and I felt my own excitement rising.

Nico was watching my face, smiling. 'I told you it was a great venue.'

'There's got to be less than three hundred people here and The Droids are massive,' I breathed, staring around in awe. 'How did you manage to get tickets?'

'My dad knows a few people,' he replied vaguely. 'Fancy a drink?'

I hesitated. Did he mean alcohol? Maybe a trumped-up library card wasn't the only fake ID he had in his back pocket. 'Er . . . yes, please.'

He raised an enquiring eyebrow. 'So what do you want?'

I didn't know what to say. If I asked for a Coke would I come across as childish? Or would he be shocked if I demanded something stronger? 'Surprise me.'

He flicked his fringe out of his eyes and his mouth quirked at the edges. 'You might regret saying that.'

I watched him weave his way towards the bar on the other side of the room, wondering what he meant. I wasn't worried he'd spike my drink; somehow I doubted he was the type who needed to get girls drunk to get them interested, but he was on his home ground and I had no idea what he was used to doing.

The support act wasn't half bad. I'd never heard of them, but I found myself swaying along to the thudding bass line with the rest of the audience. It wasn't until the band launched into their fifth song that it dawned on me how long Nico had been gone and I started to peer over the heads of the crowd. There was no sign of him. Telling myself the bar would be mobbed, I forced myself to concentrate on the stage, but I couldn't help glancing around. Out of the corner of my eye, I could see a group of older lads watching me and nudging each other. Ignoring them, I focused on the band. If Nico wasn't back by the end of the song, I'd ring him.

'What's a nice girl like you doing in a place like this?'

The words were practically bellowed into my ear and made me jump. I turned to see who had spoken. It was one of the boys from the group who'd been watching me. 'Sorry?' I said.

The boy grinned. Up close I could see he was much

older than me, probably eighteen or nineteen. He'd been drinking too, I could smell it on his breath.

'I think you're well fit. Are you here on your own?'

Panic coiled in my stomach and I willed Nico to come back. 'No, I'm here with a friend.'

He grinned unpleasantly and shifted so close to me that I could feel the heat radiating from his body. 'Great! Is she fit too?'

'Sorry to disappoint you, mate, but she's with me.' Nico materialised beside me and my breath whooshed out in a relieved sigh.

The boy raised his head in challenge, but whatever he saw in Nico's face made him think again. 'No problem,' he muttered and slunk back to his friends.

'I can't leave you alone for five minutes, can I?' Nico observed with a slight shake of his head. He thrust a condensation-covered glass of dark liquid towards me. 'Sorry I was so long, the bar was heaving.'

I sniffed at the glass cautiously. Was it vodka that was odourless, or gin?

'It's just Coke, Skye,' Nico said, amusement etched on his face. 'I'm not trying to get you drunk.'

My face flushed. 'I didn't think you were.'

He threw me a disbelieving look. 'Yeah, you did, but it's OK. Some of the lads at school would definitely try it, and you don't know that much about me yet.'

Sipping my drink, I waited for the heat to drain from

my face. When I felt calm again, I tapped his arm and pointed at the stage. 'They're good.'

Nico nodded. 'Wait until The Droids come on. This place will go mental.'

A twinge of pain shot up my leg as my ankle complained about carrying my weight and I realised wearing my high-heeled boots had been a mistake, no matter how many precious centimetres they added to my height. I winced. Immediately, Nico placed a hand under my arm to steady me. 'Do you want to find a seat?'

The pain hadn't been bad, but I didn't want to make things any worse and be forced to miss the main event. 'If that's OK?'

We made our way to the back of the room and stopped. There were no seats, but beside the wall was an empty stretch of floor. 'Down there?' I mouthed, pointing, and Nico gave me the thumbs-up.

I slid to the floor, rotating my ankle gently. It wasn't hurting that much, but I was glad to sit down. Nico settled beside me, his long legs resting next to mine.

It was quieter back there and Nico didn't have to shout to make himself heard. 'So how come you transferred to Heath Park?'

My home life wasn't something I talked about much, but the question was innocent enough. 'My mum is studying in Australia for a year so I'm living with my aunt.'

His eyes were black pools in the subdued lighting. 'No dad?'

Again, it was a reasonable question and I answered truthfully. 'No. He died before I was born.'

He didn't look away like most people do when I tell them about my dad. Instead, he paused before saying, 'My mum died when I was a kid.'

He was the only other person I'd met my age with a dead parent. Loads of kids were in one-parent families but no one else's mum or dad had died. I stared into his inky gaze, feeling the connection between us strengthen. 'It sucks, doesn't it?'

'Yeah. The worst bit is that I hardly know anything about her. My dad never mentions her.'

I could so identify with that. Dad was a closed book as far as Mum was concerned. Sometimes, I wondered if he'd ever visited me as a ghost, but he'd never identified himself if he had so I guessed he was at peace. My heart went out to Nico. Losing your dad was hard but growing up motherless had to be worse. Maybe that was why he'd sounded so bitter when he'd mentioned his dad.

I leaned closer and laid a hand on his arm. 'I'm sure she's happy, wherever she is.'

'I guess. I don't tell many people about her.' Nico gazed down at my upturned face for a moment, his expression growing in intensity. 'There's something about you I can't figure out,' he whispered, edging his head towards mine. 'It's like you have this secret you can't share with anyone. Do you?'

The words rang the faintest of alarm bells in the back of my mind, but they were lost in the sea of his closeness. All I could picture was his mouth, millimetres from mine, and how it would feel if I reached up to brush his lips with my own.

'No,' I whispered back and my skin tingled as it all but touched him.

Smiling, he murmured, 'We all have secrets. What's yours, Skye?'

He inched closer. My eyelids started to drift shut in heightened anticipation and I forced them open. I wanted to see him as our mouths met. I wanted to know if the lightning bolt about to blast me affected him the same way.

It felt like an eternity we hovered there, our breath mingling together, oblivious to anyone or anything else around us. There was no crowd, there was no band, it was just the two of us about to do something magical. When he finally closed the gap and lowered his mouth to mine, I thought I was going to explode. My eyes drifted closed, no longer under my control. Gently, his lips parted mine and I pressed against him, every nerve in my body tingling.

It felt like hours had passed when we broke apart, but I knew it could only have been seconds. Unsteadily, I opened my eyes and looked deep into his. They were even more shadowy than usual. The softest of smiles curled around his mouth. 'You're full of surprises, Skye Thackery.'

I smiled back and leaned in for another kiss. 'Trust me, you have no idea.'

Chapter 11

You know when you're looking forward to something but dreading it at the same time? After Nico had walked me home from the gig and we'd stopped under practically every tree along my road to check we hadn't forgotten how to snog, I'd almost floated through Sunday. Even Mary's blatantly disapproving glowers weren't enough to bring me down. It served her right if she'd seen more than she'd bargained for – she shouldn't have been spying on me. But Monday morning brought a cold dose of reality. Nico and I hadn't discussed how we were going to handle things at school. I thought we were officially going out but maybe he didn't agree? How would my classmates react? More importantly, what would Ellie do?

I already knew how Megan felt about it – she'd

snuck out of her little sister's birthday party on Sunday afternoon to pump me for every last detail on MSN. I swear I could hear her shrieks of excitement all the way from her house.

'Have you seen him yet?' she hissed as I joined the line for morning registration outside our classroom. 'Ellie is going to implode when she finds out!'

'Which is why I'd rather she didn't until I've had a chance to speak to Nico,' I whispered back, casting an uneasy glance over Megan's shoulder at the back of Ellie's glossy head. 'Maybe it was just a one-night thing.'

Megan rolled her eyes. 'Oh, please. You can't keep away from each other, of course it wasn't a one-night thing.' She pursed her lips mischievously and opened her mouth to sing. 'He looooves yooou!'

'Shhh!' I whacked her arm to shut her up, but it was too late. Ellie was watching us through narrowed eyes.

'What's going on, freak?'

I threw Megan a 'thanks very much' look. 'Nothing.'

Ellie stepped closer. 'I hope you aren't getting any ideas about Nico. He's only bothering with you because he feels sorry for you, that's all.'

'Oh yeah?' Megan chipped in smugly before I could say anything. 'He feels so sorry for her that he asked her out and then snogged her face off all night, did he?'

I glared at Megan, but she just shrugged. So much for keeping things quiet.

Ellie's expression could have soured milk. 'I don't believe it.'

'Ask him yourself, then,' Megan smirked. 'He's coming now.'

My heart leaped crazily in my chest and I turned round. Megan was right, Nico was heading towards us.

Ellie didn't waste any time. 'Hi, Nico,' she purred up at him. 'You know, if you're looking for company I wouldn't mind . . .'

Her voice trailed off as Nico completely ignored her. Eyes intent on me, he closed the distance and, in one fluid movement, bent his head to mine and kissed me.

The corridor fell silent as I slid my arms around his neck and lost myself once again. Then I heard Mr Exton clearing his throat. 'Albescu. This isn't the time or the place.'

Sniggers broke out around us and we broke apart. Nico flashed a private smile at me. 'See you later?'

Dazed, I nodded and watched as he made his way down the corridor. Ellie was staring after him, her mouth open. Megan reached out a finger and pushed it shut.

'Well, that answers that question,' she said, grinning in satisfaction. 'Definitely not a one-night thing.'

'Can I ask you something?' I said.

It was early evening and daylight had long since faded. Nico and I were snuggled together on a bench at the top of Parliament Hill, Hampstead Heath sprawling below us and the lights of London twinkling like fireflies in the distance. It had been two blissful weeks since he'd kissed me at school and although we hadn't dared to do that again, we'd seen each other every day. He was everything I'd hoped he'd be and I was starting to wonder if I could trust him with my secret.

'What do you want to know?'

I wriggled around until I could see his face. 'How old were you when your mum died?'

I felt his arms tighten around me, then relax. 'Around three. Why?'

'I never even knew my dad. Do you remember your mum much?'

He thought for a moment. 'Not really. I remember snatches, here and there. An old Romanian nursery rhyme she used to sing, the way she smelled of baking and roses – that kind of thing. But I don't know what she looked like.'

Nico hardly talked about his family at all, apart from when he needed to get away to do a job for his father. I hadn't really noticed, because I kept the details of my home life pretty quiet too. But Megan had been quizzing me about him and had been surprised by how little I knew.

'He's the love of your life and you don't know his dad's name or what he does?' she'd said, eyebrows raised.

'I know Charlie's mum's middle name and we're not even going out.'

I'd stared at her, wondering how she could possibly have found that out. 'Well, no.'

'Aren't you curious? I would be, especially since Nico works for him.'

Her words had made me wonder why Nico didn't talk about his family. I had a good reason for my silence; what was his?

A man walked past the bench with a chocolate Labrador on a long lead. It bounded towards us, snuffling at Nico's outstretched hand with enthusiastic snorts. The man tugged it away, apologising. Once they'd gone, I went on, 'If you could talk to her, what would you say?'

Shrugging, he said, 'I'd tell her not to worry.'

I blinked. I'd been expecting him to say something about missing her. 'Why would she be worried?'

He tensed again. 'Something my dad said once. Forget it.'

Chewing at a fingernail, I wondered what he meant. I supposed it was natural for a mother to worry about her son if she wasn't there to care for him, but something about the way Nico had said it made me think he'd thought about it a lot. I also sensed it was a sensitive subject and one I'd better steer clear of for now. Besides, I had my own agenda. 'Do you believe in life after death?'

He didn't answer straight away. 'Like heaven and hell, you mean?'

'Kind of,' I said slowly. 'Some people think their spirit lingers after they've died.'

He looked straight into my eyes then. 'You're talking about ghosts.'

My pulse sped up as I debated whether or not to carry on. If I stopped now, I could laugh it off, pretend I hadn't meant ghosts at all. But I knew I wasn't going to stop. 'Yeah. Have you ever seen one?'

I held my breath, waiting for the laughter. It didn't come. Instead, Nico reached out a hand to stroke my cheek. 'I haven't, but I know people who have. According to them, there are ghosts everywhere.'

My eyes widened as I stared back at him. 'Maybe they're right.'

His dark eyes glittered in the rising moonlight. 'How would you know? Unless you've seen one?'

This was it; I stood on the edge of the cliff. If I stepped from safety, I'd be trusting him more than I'd ever trusted anyone. I couldn't read anything in his expression. He was waiting for me to go on. Breathing in uneven gulps, I whispered, 'I see them all the time.'

For a few long seconds, he didn't move. Then a faint smile crossed his face. 'I thought so.'

My jaw dropped. It wasn't the reply I'd expected. 'You thought so? What does that mean?'

'It was the only explanation that made sense.' Wrapping his arms more tightly around me, he planted a kiss on my nose. 'You're clearly not schizophrenic and I always knew you weren't talking to yourself when I overheard you in the hall at school. So it was obvious you were talking to someone I couldn't see.'

My head was spinning. He'd known I was lying about the mental illness? 'But how is that the obvious conclusion?'

He looked away, his face pensive as though debating something. Then he gazed at me again. 'I've never told anyone this, but my dad is psychic. Not in the same way that you are, but he can talk to the dead.'

I couldn't believe what I was hearing. Psychic ability ran in families, so —

'I'm not psychic,' Nico said, reading my mind. 'Not yet, anyway.'

'Not yet?' I echoed, perplexed. It was hardly something you went to college to become.

He frowned slightly. 'I can't tell you much, but my dad has some . . . friends who can teach me how to do it.'

Alarm bells rang. Pulling away, I fixed him with a hard look. 'What kind of friends?'

'Don't worry, they're not into anything bad. They just know how to contact the dead.'

I'd heard about people who made claims like this before. In every single case, they'd been fraudsters. 'Nico —'

'Don't worry, it's cool,' he soothed, drawing me close. 'They're practically my family, back in Romania. I've known them all my life.'

I let him kiss me but it didn't work its usual magic. Instead, his words whirled around my brain and I couldn't shake a deep feeling of concern. Friends who claimed to speak to ghosts – what kind of family did Nico come from? Then again, I was hardly in a position to judge; I didn't exactly come from a conventional background myself.

Nico ended the kiss, leaning back so he could see me clearly. 'There's something else I have to tell you. I'm going away for a while, with my dad.'

Dismayed, I bit my lip. 'How long for?'

'I don't know. A week, maybe? He's got something he needs to do back home and he needs my help.'

Megan was right; I should be wondering what Nico's dad did for a living but it didn't seem like the right time to ask. 'In Romania?'

Nodding, he said, 'Yeah, just a bit of business he needs to take care of. I'll be back before you even miss me.'

Somehow, I doubted that. I slipped my arms around him. 'I wish you weren't going.'

He hugged me close, turning his face away to breathe in the cold night air. 'I won't be gone long and when I get back we might have something else in common.'

Troubled, I didn't reply. What if these so-called friends weren't con-men but something more sinister? I'd never met anyone who dabbled in dark arts, but I knew they existed. Nico had no idea what he might be getting into.

'Thank you for trusting me, Skye,' he whispered into my hair. 'I love you for it.'

His lips found mine before I could speak. Confused, I tried to make sense of my feelings. Nico had just told me he loved me; I ought to be elated. Instead, I couldn't shake off a chill as I wondered about the things he wasn't telling me. Then his mouth became more insistent and I pushed my fears to one side. I'd shared my deepest secret with him and he didn't think I was crazy. He'd trusted me too, and maybe I was overreacting; hadn't he said his friends were like family? They'd have his welfare at heart, and surely his dad wouldn't let anything bad happen. There was more to the story, but I didn't push. Nico would tell me when he was ready. Closing my eyes, I returned the kiss hungrily. Nico and I were perfect together. Nothing could spoil that.

Chapter 12

'I think I've discovered the identity of our mystery jumper.'

Since he'd found out he could see the suicide ghost from Hornsey Lane Bridge, Jeremy had been trying to work out who she was. Celestine had been mystified about why he could see some ghosts and not others, but Mary had claimed the clues were hidden in his past, which had earned blank looks all round. And now Jeremy was waving a sheet of paper in my face and looking pleased with himself.

Letting out an annoyed grunt, I shifted sideways, my gaze fixed on the television. 'You make her sound like a cardigan.'

Undeterred by my grumpiness, he sat beside me and started to read. 'Isobel Mitchell, aged thirty-seven, committed suicide by throwing herself off Hornsey Lane Bridge on 30th November 1998.'

I wasn't in the mood to congratulate him. 'Why?'

Jeremy scanned the paper again. 'It doesn't say. She didn't leave a note.' He placed the sheet on the coffee table in front of me. 'But I imagine she was very depressed.'

I exhaled loudly. 'Do you think so, Sherlock?'

My sarcasm was apparently wasted on him. 'Yes, I do,' he said. 'So how are we going to help her?'

I didn't have the faintest idea. Since Nico had gone three days earlier, I'd found it hard to summon up the energy to care about anything. Megan had done her best to distract me and Dontay had called round a few times, but I hadn't exactly been sparkling company, and on his last visit he'd said he was giving me some space. I knew Celestine was worried about me, but other than to gently ask if there was anything she could do to help, she'd left me alone. Jeremy, on the other hand, seemed to be constantly trying to take my mind off things and it was starting to get on my nerves. 'I don't know.'

'When I was helping Lucy, we tracked down some-one else her killer had attacked,' Jeremy said.

And that was another thing about Jeremy, I decided as he droned on in the background: it felt like he went on about Lucy all the time. I mean, I know she was the first ghost he'd seen – the *only* one he'd seen before Isobel – and she had obviously meant a lot to him, but did he have to mention her like twenty times a day?

'Well, since the only person Isobel killed was herself, I don't think it's going to help in this case.' My voice sounded petulant and childish, but I couldn't stop. 'Maybe if Lucy was still here she'd have some brilliant idea about what to do, but she isn't, OK?'

His gaze was steady. 'I'm just trying to help, Skye.'

'Don't bother,' I snapped and stood up. Anger coursed through me and sought the nearest available target. 'There's not much we can do, anyway.'

I pushed past him and stamped up the stairs, slamming the door to my room and throwing myself on the bed. Hot, miserable tears spilled down my cheeks as my harsh words replayed themselves in my head. Great, now I felt mean as well as heartbroken. It hadn't been fair to talk to Jeremy that way; he was only trying to help, and he didn't really go on about Lucy that much.

Celestine tapped on my door fifteen minutes later. 'Skye? Can I come in?'

Grabbing a tissue, I wiped the worst of the tears from my face and blew my nose. 'Yeah,' I called in a subdued tone, sounding like I had a peg on my nose.

She pushed back the door and watched me for a moment. 'Jeremy told me what happened. Is there something you want to talk about?'

I shredded the soggy tissue between my fingernails. 'Not really.'

Picking her way across the piles of clothes on the floor, she came and sat on the edge of my unmade bed. 'Did something happen at school? Have you fallen out with Nico?'

Fresh tears pooled up in my eyes and suddenly it was all spilling out of me; how Nico didn't think I was weird, what he'd told me on Parliament Hill about his trip to Romania and how I was worried that he might be involved with psychic charlatans or worse. Celestine didn't say a word until I'd finished, then she sat back and studied me, concern written all over her face.

'I'm not surprised you're feeling terrible,' she said finally. 'You poor thing.'

I sniffled, with more than a touch of self pity.

'But that's no excuse for taking it out on the rest of us,' she went on. 'We all have feelings, even ghosts. Especially the ghosts – poor Dontay asked me tonight if he'd done something to upset you.'

Guilt squeezed at my stomach. My problems were nothing compared to his. 'I'm sorry,' I mumbled. 'It's all got so messed up.'

'When is Nico back?'

And that was another source of concern: I hadn't heard from him since he'd gone. Pressing my lips together, I swallowed another wave of tears. 'I don't know. He's not answering my texts.'

Celestine gripped my hands in reassurance. 'I'm

sure he'll be back soon.'

She was right, of course, but it didn't stop me missing him.

'Do you think his friends are really psychic?' I asked. Half of me hoped she'd laugh. She didn't.

'I don't know. Romanian folklore has strong links with the supernatural, and there are some well-respected psychics from the Carpathian Mountains, but they don't claim to be able to teach the ability to communicate with the dead. I doubt these friends are even really gifted, so let's hope Nico's dad is smart enough to avoid getting hustled.'

Nico had sounded pretty convinced that it wasn't a con. 'Yeah, you're probably right.'

Standing up, Celestine glanced around at the mess before smiling down at me. 'So, do you think you might owe Jeremy an apology?'

I bit back a sigh; she had a point. 'Yeah, in a minute.'

'Good,' she replied. 'If you really wanted to help, you could go and see the ghost on the bridge with him.'

I wanted to tell her that I had enough on my plate with Dontay, but I didn't. 'OK.' Then something occurred to me. 'Hey, does this mean I get a lift to school everyday?'

Celestine's eyes twinkled. 'Do you know, I think it just might.'

* * *

I apologised to Dontay too, when I went to the Dearly D on Thursday evening. He shrugged it off, of course, and acted like he hadn't even noticed my foul mood. I was grateful he understood; some of my old friends wouldn't have.

'It's cool,' he said, once we were sitting on the wall opposite the church. 'And we don't have to be around each other twenty-four seven. You got friends to see, I get that. Nigel or whatever his name is.'

I shivered as a drop of icy rain squirmed down my neck. It was pouring down and my little umbrella was taking a serious pounding. 'He's gone away.'

'How come?'

I sighed. 'Family stuff.'

My misery must have been obvious because Dontay growled, 'You need me to have a word when he gets back?'

The thought might have made me giggle if it wasn't for Nico's belief he'd soon be talking to ghosts. Anxiety ran through me and I shivered. 'Nah, it's OK. How's Nelson?'

A heavy scowl creased Dontay's face. 'Him talking about Shank the other day worried me, so I decided to follow him.' He shook his head in disgust. 'It turns out he's been missing training, going off to do stuff for the other gang members.'

A gust of wind buffeted me sideways. 'What kind of stuff?'

Dontay's scowl deepened. 'It starts off with something small. "Just deliver this package" they'll say, but you don't know what's under the paper and it's worth more than your life to look. If you do a good job then they'll trust you with something else.' He paused. 'It feels good at first, being part of it, but then they ask you to do something a bit shady, steaming probably, to prove your loyalty.'

'Steaming?' I repeated, wrinkling my nose in puzzlement. The only steaming I could think of was the kind you did with an iron and I didn't think the London Fields Posse were running a laundry service.

'It's where a load of you run through a crowd, nicking people's phones and wallets. Before you know it, you're running from the law, and there's no way out cos then the gang have got something on you.'

'Oh.' I stared at him. 'Is that what happened to you?'

He threw me a scornful look. 'Nah. I didn't do nothing illegal. Not much anyway. How could I when I had Nelson looking up to me?' He sighed and gave a small shrug. 'But I suppose I played the game a bit, stayed on the edges. I was too smart to get caught up in it.'

'But Nelson isn't that smart?'

'I didn't say that,' he muttered, but I could tell that was exactly what he'd meant. 'It's complicated.'

'Try me.'

'He's all messed up in here.' He tapped the side of his

head. 'When I died, he changed. It's like he stopped being my kid brother and turned into this person I don't know. I think he wants revenge for my death.'

A chill settled over me, and it wasn't just from the rain trickling down my neck. 'Do you think that's why he's joined the gang?'

He nodded and I caught a flash of fear behind his eyes. 'For sure. But he's just a kid, he doesn't get that Shank is using him, and my parents have no idea what he's into. Shank has filled his head with the idea that he's got to step up and avenge me. I'm scared he'll end up in a really bad place – maybe even get himself killed.'

His words stayed with me all the way home. The thought of Nelson getting in over his head and dying for something nobody wanted made me feel physically sick. My worries over Nico were tiny by comparison; Nelson's future and maybe his life were hanging in the balance, for crying out loud. But as scared as Dontay had made me feel, I knew I'd do whatever I could to help. I'd just have to hope that when it came down to it, Dontay had my back. Because one thing was for sure: I couldn't save his brother on my own.

Chapter 13

'Are you sure you want to do this?'

It was Jeremy's night off and we were sitting in the car, watching Hornsey Lane Bridge to see if Isobel showed up. We'd seen her a couple more times on the way to school, but I'd always been late and we hadn't stopped. Now we had plenty of time, but no ghost.

Jeremy sighed. 'I can think of several things I'd rather be doing, actually, but the thought of Isobel keeps nagging at me. She reminds me of Hep, Lucy's friend.'

I thought back to the conversation we'd had the day he first saw Isobel. 'She killed herself too, right?'

'Yes, but I don't think she really meant to. The saddest thing about Hep was that if she'd had some-one to talk to when she was still alive, her problems might have been sorted out.'

'What happened to her?'

He gazed out of the window. 'Lucy and I helped her to make peace with her parents and she passed across. I wonder if we can do something similar for Isobel.'

We sat in silence for a minute, watching the occasional pedestrian cross the bridge. Not for the first time, I considered how lucky it had been that Jeremy and my aunt had found each other. I could imagine how freaked out he'd been when he'd first seen Lucy and had no one he could talk to about it. For Celestine, it must help if your other half understood what you were going through. 'You really cared about Lucy and Hep.'

Smiling, he nodded. 'If you'd asked me a year ago if I'd be hanging around a toilet with a copy of *Heat* so a girl no one else saw could read it, I'd have laughed. Actually, I'd have thought you were mad. But as soon I saw how lonely she was, I couldn't walk away. I think Isobel might be the same.'

A movement out of the corner of my eye caught my attention and I squinted through the windscreen. 'Now's your chance to find out – she's over there. We'll have to be quick, it looks like she's getting ready to jump.'

He was out of the car in seconds. 'Isobel, wait!'

She paused in the act of climbing on to the parapet and turned her head to listen. 'Who's there?'

'My name's Jeremy,' he called. I slammed the car door

and stood behind him. 'This is Skye. We're here to help you.'

'You can't,' Isobel dismissed and resumed her climb. 'I'm beyond help.'

I thought that was a bit melodramatic, but Jeremy hurried forwards. 'Look, we only want to talk to you for a few minutes. If you still want to jump at the end, you can.' He stopped at the edge of the pavement. 'What have you got to lose?'

Isobel seemed to be considering his words. Then she clambered down. 'No one's ever tried to stop me before,' she said, turning to face us. 'In fact, I don't think anyone knows I'm here.'

'We're psychic,' I explained. 'We see ghosts all the time. Or at least I do. Jeremy only sees one or two.'

Isobel looked at him. 'And I'm one of them?'

Nodding, he said, 'Yes.'

'Why?'

'I don't know,' he said. 'But I do want to try to help you, if I can. Why do you jump off this bridge every day?'

She sniffed. 'I don't have anything better to do.'

Jeremy and I exchanged glances. It looked like Isobel was going to be hard work.

'Yes, but why are you doing it over and over again? Are you angry? Sad? Both of those things?'

I thought for a minute she was going to bolt, but I guess the chance to tell her story was too great to pass up. She fixed him with a piercing stare. 'You really want to know? How long have you got?'

After that, there was no stopping her. Soon, we knew the whole sorry tale: how she'd lost her job in the City and become depressed, how her husband had left her for another woman and finally, how she'd lost her home because she couldn't keep up the mortgage repayments and it felt like no one cared. It made depressing listening and I didn't have a clue what to say at the end. Jeremy did, though. 'You've been through a terrible time. Didn't you have any family you could turn to?'

Isobel shook her head. 'My parents are both dead and my friends kept telling me things would get better. But nothing ever did.'

'And so you jumped?'

'I thought it would be over,' she said, heaving a sigh. 'Instead, I'm stuck here.'

Jeremy smiled encouragingly. 'Well, at least you've got us now.'

Her expression brightened. 'Really? You'll come back?'

'Of course we will. And we'll introduce you to other ghosts too.'

'There's a whole afterlife for you to discover,' I chipped in, but she didn't seem to hear me. Her gaze was glued to Jeremy.

'When? When are you coming back? Tomorrow?'

He hesitated, then nodded. 'Sure, we can come back tomorrow if you like.'

Isobel's eyes glistened. 'Thank you. It means so much to me. You've changed my life.'

I supposed she was right, watching her giggle at Jeremy's jokes. But there was something familiar about the way she was eyeing him. It bothered me all the way home and it wasn't until I was getting into bed that I realised what it was. Isobel hadn't behaved with Jeremy the way ghosts usually acted around psychics; Isobel had looked at Jeremy the way that Ellie looked at Nico.

I didn't mention my worries to Jeremy. Maybe I'd got it wrong, anyway, and Isobel was just grateful for his attention. She was certainly keen, waiting for us to drive by every morning and waggling her fingers at him as we did. By the time Friday rolled around, even Celestine was raising an eyebrow at the amount of Jeremy's time Isobel was taking up.

'Have you told her about the Dearly D?' she asked over breakfast.

Jeremy nodded. 'Yes, but she doesn't feel ready to go yet. She says she wants to get to know me better first.'

I snorted into my Weetabix. It was the clearest sign yet that Isobel had developed a crush on Jeremy.

Celestine frowned. 'It sounds like she's becoming a bit dependent on you. I think you should encourage her to go to the Dearly D. Find something from the bridge she can take with her. Maybe then she'll realise you're not the answer to all her problems.'

'She's only being friendly,' he said. 'I'm sure she'll want to meet other ghosts soon.'

I looked at Celestine and shrugged. I hoped for Jeremy's sake he was right; hell had no fury like a spirit scorned.

I got to Friday evening without any further mishaps. I still hadn't heard from Nico and I tried not to fret. Over a Big Mac and fries, which I ate as Dontay tried not to drool, we came up with a loose plan to get Nelson's attention, and on Saturday morning we headed to the pitches at Hackney Marshes to pull everything together before Nelson turned up to play. It was so early that the fields were empty, apart from the occasional dog walker or jogger, so I had no worries about looking like a lunatic talking to myself. The problem was that the plan involved ball skills I didn't have, and Dontay wasn't turning out to be the most patient teacher.

'No, use your knees!' he yelled at me as the ball bounced away over the sodden ground for what felt like the millionth time. 'They're called keep-ups, not drop-downs.'

'Ha ha,' I mumbled, picking it up and pushing my bedraggled fringe out of my eyes. 'It would help if you could show me how it's done instead of shouting at me.'

He glared at me. 'Very funny. You just control the ball. It's easy.'

I threw the ball towards him. It rolled a few metres past him and bobbled to a stop. 'If it's so easy why don't you show me?'

'How am I supposed to do that? I'm a ghost, remember?'

Hands on hips, I returned his glare. 'You just control the ball, it's easy.'

We stood glowering at each other for a few seconds. Then his shoulders slumped. 'Stop tormenting me. You know how much I'd give to be able to play again.'

My own expression softened and I felt bad, but not bad enough to let him off the hook. 'Then try. Other ghosts can touch things. How do you think poltergeists manage to move stuff around?'

'I've never thought about it,' he admitted. 'What do I have to do?'

I knew that most ghosts used anger or some other strong emotion to allow them to make contact with non-ghostly objects. Given the way Dontay had just been bellowing at me, fury shouldn't be too hard to manage.

'You need to get angry,' I advised. 'Then try to push it with your finger.'

Looking anything but convinced, he knelt beside the ball and thrust a finger towards it. Nothing happened.

He wasn't feeling enough emotion, I decided. 'You don't look very angry to me. Are you sure you want this?'

Ignoring me, he stabbed his hand towards the ball again. Still nothing happened.

There were signs of movement on some of the other pitches. The teams were starting to arrive and we were running out of time. I summoned up my most jeering tones. 'I thought you were supposed to be good at this? You can't even pick up the ball!'

Dontay scowled furiously at me. 'In case you hadn't noticed, it's called football, not handball.'

'So kick it, then!' I yelled and dredged my mind for football phrases. 'Bend it like Beckham!'

In a burst of rage, he lashed out his foot. It connected firmly with the ball, sending it soaring through the air and on to the neighbouring pitch. We stared at in stunned silence for a minute.

'So,' I said in a tentative voice. 'How did that feel?'

'Almost as good as it used to be.' Dontay flashed me a tiny grin. 'What was with that Beckham stuff?'

My cheeks turned pink. 'It was the only thing I could think of to say. It worked, anyway – think you can do it again?'

His grin almost split his face it was so wide. 'Are you serious? Now I know how to do it I'm never gonna stop!'

Which could be a bit of a problem, I thought, as he raced towards the ball. People tended to get a bit freaked out by things apparently moving around on their own. And it could be exhausting to do it for long periods of time. I needed him fresh if our plan was going to work.

'Wait for me!' I called and jogged after him. 'I can't do this without you.'

By the time Nelson and his team-mates arrived at the Marshes, I'd learned a lot. I'm not saying that I was ready for Skill School or anything, but thanks to Dontay's teaching I could manage at least to keep the ball under control. Dontay had mastered touching physical objects with incredible speed; I guessed his talent for football had helped. All I needed now was to use my newfound talent to get Nelson's attention.

I knew that he'd clocked me standing on the touch-line almost straight away, but he didn't acknowledge me until half-time. I stood to one side of the pitch, practising bouncing the ball off my knees and trainers, just as Dontay had showed me. Nelson jogged over to me, his gaze suspicious.

'You again.'

'Hi, Nelson,' I said absently, concentrating on keeping the ball in the air.

'What are you doing here?'

'Playing keep-ups, what does it look like?'

In my desperation to look like I knew what I was

doing, I gave a particularly energetic thrust of my knee. The ball bounced high and I knew I was going to lose it, but then Dontay was beside me. With a flick of his leg and a look of intense concentration, he brought the ball under control and sailing back towards my foot. I stuck out a muddy trainer and the ball landed obediently on it. Dontay winked.

I slid Nelson a sideways look. 'Fancy a game?' Then I blushed. What if he thought I was chatting him up?

Sure enough, his eyebrows shot up. 'Nah. I'm in the middle of a match.'

Surreptitiously, I tried to fan my blushing cheeks. 'Afterwards, then? Or are you scared of getting beaten by a girl?'

He shrugged. 'Fine. If you want to get your arse kicked, it's no skin off my nose.'

He turned and went back to his team. As he reached them he said something and they all turned to look at me. I was so busy trying to watch them out of the corner of my eye that the ball once again spun out of control and this time not even Dontay's skills could rescue it. As it flew upwards and over my head, I heard Nelson and his friends laugh.

'This had better be worth it,' I told Dontay through gritted teeth as I picked up the ball and started again. 'This had so better be worth it.'

* * *

The jibe about losing to a girl must have really hurt Nelson, because he showed me absolutely no mercy. A few of his team-mates had come over to watch after their match was over, and if I hadn't had Dontay beside me, flicking and nudging the ball, I'd have lost almost as soon as the game began. I couldn't believe how good he was; two hours earlier he hadn't even been able to even touch the ball and now he was giving Cristiano Ronaldo a run for his money. His skill was unnatural; he must have been some footballer before he died.

Dontay stood so close to me that we were practically touching. I knew it must be as uncomfortable for him as it was for me; Mary never stopped moaning about how unpleasant it was to have someone walk through you. But it worked like a charm, and by the time Nelson and I were both panting through the exertion, he was looking at me with new respect.

'You're not bad,' he said when we stopped to catch our breath. 'For a girl.'

Dontay shook his head in mock embarrassment. 'Our mum would go nuts if she heard him say stuff like that.'

'Yeah, well I had a good teacher,' I replied, without thinking. 'Your brother.'

Nelson stared at me. 'Dontay taught you to play keep-ups? I thought you said you met him down the snooker hall.'

I blushed. 'Er . . . we did. But then he showed me some of his other skills.'

Sniggers broke out among Nelson's mates.

'I bet he did,' one of them called out.

'It wasn't like that,' I insisted, keeping my eyes trained on Nelson. 'We were mates, that's all.'

Nelson looked like he didn't believe me. 'Like I said, he never told me about you.'

'He told me plenty about you,' I said, lowering my voice. 'Like how you're going to be a great footballer and play for West Ham someday.' I paused and waited until he returned my gaze. 'How proud he was of you for staying on the straight and narrow.'

There was an awkward silence. Then Nelson spoke, 'Yeah, well.'

The other boys started shuffling around. The one who'd made the joke about Dontay showing me his skills waved a hand. 'Nelson, man, I'm off. See ya.'

The others took that as their cue to go as well, leaving Nelson staring at the pitch and me wondering where to go from here.

'He wouldn't want you to go looking for revenge,' I said once we were alone, deciding on the direct approach.

Nelson looked up angrily. 'How do you know? He was murdered by them Marsh Street scum and no one cared. The police talked about catching the shooter but they never did nothing about it. Who else is going to sort it out if I don't?'

I glanced towards Dontay anxiously. 'Don't get involved with the gangs. You'll just get hurt and Dontay doesn't want that.'

Nelson shrugged dismissively. 'Shank won't let that happen. He looks after his own.' He fixed me with an accusing stare. 'Why are you talking about my brother like he was still here?'

Realising there was only one way out, I took a deep breath. 'Maybe he is.'

Disgust etched itself over his face as he backed off. 'You're a nutter. Keep away from me, yeah?'

'That went well,' I mumbled to Dontay as his brother stamped across the pitch.

'That wasn't him talking,' Dontay said, his voice flat. 'That's the sort of thing Shank would say. They're building him up to do a shooting and using me as an excuse.'

I shivered, and it wasn't due to the sweat drying on my skin. 'Then we have to find out when and where. Because if you ask me, Nelson seems plenty angry enough to do something he's going to regret.'

Chapter 14

Celestine folded her arms and threw me an adamant look. 'No. Absolutely not.'

I slumped on to the sofa and sighed. 'Why not? All I have to do is find out where the gang leader is, set Mary on him, and Nelson will be safe. Actually, we'd be doing the whole world a favour.'

She held up a finger. 'One, Mary is not an evil spirit.' Considering some of the stunts she'd pulled on me I had severe doubts about that, but I kept my mouth shut and Celestine went on. 'Two, it goes against everything spiritualism stands for to use ghosts to get something you want. And three, it's too dangerous. What if he's so terrified he takes it out on the living?'

OK, so I hadn't thought of that, but it still wasn't the worst plan in the world. And I couldn't see another way of preventing Nelson from getting himself into a situation where it was kill or be killed. 'What do you suggest, then?'

'I could talk to his parents, make them aware of what's going on?'

I shook my head. 'I suggested that. Dontay says it wouldn't work. They'd try to ban Nelson from going out and he'd become even more devious. Anything else?'

Jeremy looked up from the Sunday papers. 'Have you thought about going to the police?'

'And saying what? There's a ghost who's worried his brother is going to try to avenge his death?' I snorted derisively. 'That'd go down well.'

'I think you should get them involved,' Jeremy insisted. 'They have whole departments devoted to fighting gang crime. Surely they must have an idea of what's going on.'

I shuddered at the thought of the reaction of the boys in blue. 'If you feel so strongly about it, then why don't you go and see them?'

Celestine groaned but Jeremy looked pleased. 'All right, then, I will.'

'I'd have thought you'd be too busy with Isobel to get involved with my ghostly problems, but what do I know?' I said. It was a low blow, but Isobel was driving us crazy. The moment Jeremy had given her a small lump of stone from the bridge so that she could move around, she'd taken to standing outside the house. Mary was threatening to call in an exorcist to get rid of her. 'Just don't mention Nelson by name. Dontay will go mental if his brother gets picked up. And don't drag me into it.'

I needn't have stressed over Jeremy's Sherlock Holmes tendencies – Dontay didn't bat an eyelid when I tentatively mentioned it. In fact, he looked almost pleased, much to my relief. We were at Lee Valley ice rink and Dontay was my safety net as I flailed around like Bambi on – well – ice. If he'd got the hump and left, I'd have been flat on my backside before you could say A&E.

'There's a lot of couples here,' he said, gazing round the rink and drifting sideways to avoid a speeding ice marshal. Coloured lights refracted off the frozen white ground and a slamming bass-line chased them round.

'I suppose,' I said, concentrating on sliding one wobbly skate in front of another. 'For a Sunday night, anyway.'

I'd taken Jeremy's advice and plugged a mobile phone earpiece into my ear so I could talk without looking like a care in the community case. Dontay was hovering more than normal, a few centimetres above the ice, making me feel even shorter. 'Did you and Ned ever come here?'

No, and I thanked my lucky stars we hadn't. Crazy windmill arms were not a good look on anyone. It was all right for Dontay; he didn't even have to move his feet to stay upright.

'His name is Nico,' I corrected.

Dontay watched as my skate took on a life of its own and I almost did the splits. 'Have you heard from him?'

I couldn't stop the grin from spreading over my face. 'Yeah. They're leaving Romania tomorrow.'

He stared at me. 'Leaving where?'

'Romania,' I repeated, ending on a squeak as I battled to keep my balance. Other skaters flew past, making it look so easy and scaring the pants off me with their pace. It wasn't fair; how come everyone else appeared as if they were straight from the Winter Olympics and I looked more like the comedy turn? I gave up. 'That's where he's been. Fancy a sit down?'

Dontay shrugged and we headed off the ice. I sank into one of the seats behind the Perspex sheets and loosened the laces of my skates. 'Bliss,' I said, wiggling my numb toes. 'I swear they're cutting off my circulation.'

Dontay's gaze was fixed on the skaters. 'How well do you know this Nick?'

'Why?' I said, feeling a sudden rush of defensiveness. 'He's all right.'

Actually, he was more than all right, especially at kissing, but there was such a thing as too much information.

'I overheard him talking about you,' Dontay said, not

looking at me. 'Let's just say it wasn't all sugar and spice.'

I stopped rubbing my ankles to stare at him. 'When?'

'It doesn't matter.' His expression was evasive. 'All you need to know is that he ain't no Mr Nice Guy.'

Turning to face him, I repeated, 'When?'

Dontay sighed. 'One Saturday night. After you'd been to that gig and he'd walked you home.'

My jaw dropped. 'You followed me? But I thought it was Mary!'

'Yeah, well, it weren't.' He shuffled on his seat. 'She asked me to look out for you and I didn't have nothing better to do.'

'So you thought you'd spy on me,' I said in disgust, still reeling from the thought of him watching Nico and me doing – well, I didn't want to think about what we'd been up to that night. 'Pervert.'

'It weren't like that,' he insisted, his face wretched. 'I hung back, didn't get too close or nothing. Then, when you'd gone inside, I thought I'd make sure he got back to the tube all right. That's when I heard him on the phone.'

As furious as I was, I couldn't help myself. 'What did he say?'

'Not much at first, just described you and the date. Then he told whoever it was that he didn't think you'd be up for it. He said you were too nice.'

I rolled my eyes; it was hardly *CSI: Highgate.* 'That could mean anything. Is that it?'

Dontay looked uncomfortable. 'No. He got into an argument then, saying he didn't want to be in no gang and to find someone else. And he said he wasn't going back to Romania.'

Drawing in a shallow breath, I repeated the words in my mind. Nico couldn't be in a gang. He wasn't the type, for a start. Maybe he'd meant the family friends he'd told me about. 'What gang?'

With a tiny shake of his head, Dontay said, 'The Solomons, I think he called them. I've never heard of them and I know all the London massives.'

'You're wrong,' I stated, refusing to accept what he'd said. 'He must have been talking about someone else.'

Dontay studied me. 'I don't think so, Skye. You'd better ask him about it next time you see him.'

I still couldn't get my head around the fact that he'd followed me and watched us snogging. My cheeks flushed. Suddenly, the ice seemed a lot more inviting than talking to Dontay and I laced up my skates with hurried fingers. 'I'm going back out. Coming?'

Please say no, a voice whispered in my head.

'Nah,' he replied. 'I'll watch. I could do with a laugh.'

He had to have got the wrong end of the stick, I decided as I gripped the side wall and concentrated on putting as much distance between us as possible. The

Solomons? What kind of a name was that for a gang? Nico was back in Romania, but he wasn't stupid enough to get caught up in something like that. Was he? I gnawed my lip and edged forwards. I trusted Nico, but there wasn't any harm in Googling Romanian gangs when I got home. Then I could reassure Dontay that his fears were Chinese whispers and nothing more.

A boy grabbed at my sleeve to steady himself. For a second, we both teetered, then he got his balance and shot off, flashing me a cheeky grin. I glanced over at Dontay to see him smirking in my direction. Had his last comment really been necessary? OK, so I wasn't exactly channelling a Russian figure skater right now, but I'd get better. One of the marshals whizzed in front of me and stopped in a flash of silver blades, showering my feet with frosty powder. Totally ignoring me, he grinned at a group of girls and started chatting them up.

'Show off,' I muttered under my breath and let go of the wall to navigate around him. I'd show him and everyone else; by the end of the session I'd be gliding like straighteners over frizz or die trying.

'Guess who's back?'

Megan's eyes were dancing with excitement as I slid into my seat on Monday morning and that could only mean one thing: Nico.

I winced at the pain in my bum; I had a bruise there

the size of Africa to show for my attempts at an elegant twirl the night before, but Megan's news dulled the ache. 'You've seen him?'

She nodded. 'Yep. You'd have seen him too if you'd got here on time. I think he was looking for you.'

Frowning, I made a mental note to get revenge on Mary for stealing my school tie. If I hadn't wasted ten minutes looking for it, I wouldn't have been late. Catching a lift from Jeremy was out of the question now that Isobel had taken to jumping into the car with us. But maybe it was just as well I hadn't seen Nico; I had questions to ask, not to mention a burning need to kiss him, and the corridor outside my classroom wasn't the place for either of those things. 'I'll find him later.'

Mr Exton cleared his throat, signalling he'd had enough of the chatter, and Megan reluctantly turned round to face the front. Ellie shot me a dirty look and I waggled my fingers at her. She'd said nothing since the kiss in the corridor and I knew she was on the look-out for signs that things weren't going well. When she glanced away, I allowed a tiny smile of anticipation to creep over my face. Nico was back. I couldn't wait to see him.

Megan had athletics practice at lunchtime, something that was happening more and more often now that she'd made the squad. I was sitting with a group of girls I was on nodding terms with, joining in with their conversation occasionally. Despite spending most of the day scanning the crowds for Nico, I hadn't spotted him, and I was only half listening to the chatter of the girls around me when he sauntered into the canteen. I stopped picking at the crusted-over lasagne in front of me and stared as he stopped to speak to a group of boys. Then he looked across directly at me. I stood and just about managed to fight the urge to dive across the room into his arms. Instead, I smiled and waited as he came towards me.

'Hey,' he said, a smile tugging at the corner of his mouth. 'Miss me?'

I smiled back. 'No.'

Dr Bailey was patrolling the tables and spied my empty juice carton. 'Recycling bin. Careless cartons cost lives!'

For an instant, I wondered whether Nico might have heard, but he showed no signs that he had. 'I missed you,' he said. He reached out to trail his fingers along the back of my hand and lowered his voice. 'I missed kissing you.'

His touch caused a shiver of pleasure. I fantasised briefly about snogging him there and then. 'OK, so maybe I missed you a bit.'

He grinned. 'Meet me after school? I've got something to tell you.'

I threw him a sharp look. Was it my imagination or was there was something subtly different about him? The long, floppy fringe was the same and his lips were as irresistible as ever, but something had altered, and I couldn't work out what it was. I couldn't help wondering exactly what had happened while he'd been away. My Google search had drawn a blank – if there was a gang called the Solomons in Romania, I hadn't found it. I rubbed my eyes and blinked. Maybe I was seeing things that weren't really there.

'Yeah,' I said and his pleasure made the last of my worries melt away. 'You can walk me home if you like.'

Dr Bailey had circled back to us. He stopped and stared hard at Nico. 'Yours is a dark path, boy,' he said, bushy eyebrows lowered in a disapproving frown. 'Step back before it's too late.'

My mouth fell open, but the teacher was gone before I could ask him what he meant. A dark path? I knew the sun set early, but it wouldn't be that dark when we walked home. Nico saw my puzzled expression and leaned down to whisper in my ear. 'What is it? Is there a ghost here?'

He sounded eager and I remembered the look in his eyes up on Parliament Hill when he'd talked about contacting the dead, like it was something he'd dreamed of all his life. I summoned up a strained smile. 'No. I just realised I forgot my biology homework, that's all. I'd better go and find Megan to copy hers.'

As I headed out of the canteen, I tried not to think about Dr Bailey's words. Nico might be curious about my gift, but that didn't mean he was on 'a dark path'. Why did everyone think he was up to no good?

Chapter 15

Megan was beyond excited when I told her what had happened at lunchtime. I actually thought she might insist on walking home with me and Nico, but she satisfied herself with making me promise to fill her in later.

'Everything,' she said meaningfully as she left me beside the school gates. 'I mean it.'

I waved at her and then yelped as Nico's arms snaked around me from behind. He kissed my neck. 'I hope you're not really going to tell her everything,' he teased.

'Unlikely,' I said, wriggling out of his grasp. 'But it depends on what you have to tell me.'

He smiled. 'She wouldn't believe you.'

His answer made me uneasy. Clearly something unusual had happened while he was away. We followed the crowd to the main road but as the majority of the kids turned towards the bus stops, Nico and I took one of the side streets. I quickened my pace a bit too. The route we were going would take us past the edge of Highgate Cemetery and that wasn't a pleasant place for a psychic in the daytime, let alone when dusk was falling. I was avoiding Hornsey Lane Bridge, too; the last thing I needed was Isobel pumping me for information about Jeremy.

There were still a few kids around so I opted for a safe topic. 'So, how was Romania?'

Nico sighed. 'I went to a funeral. I didn't say anything before, but there was a death in the clan, which was why we needed to go.'

'Really?' I asked, wondering why he hadn't mentioned it the night he'd told me he was going away. I also wondered at the word 'clan'. 'Who died?'

'It's hard to explain. I suppose you could call him an uncle,' he said. 'I didn't know him very well, but my dad did.'

He didn't seem upset, but I felt like I should offer some sympathy. 'Sorry.'

He shrugged. 'It's OK. After all, it's not like he's really gone.'

'Not everyone becomes a ghost, Nico.' I stopped. 'How did he die?'

He took my hand and tugged at it until I started

walking again. 'It was a car accident. He crashed in the mountains.'

'Most people pass across to the astral plane when they die. It's only the ones with unfinished business who stay.'

He smiled, but it didn't make my heart flutter the way it usually did. This smile was cold. 'It was very sudden, so I'd say he has unfinished business. Maybe he'll come to see you.'

This wasn't the way I'd expected the conversation to go. I wanted to ask him who the Solomons were and why he hadn't wanted to go back to Romania. Instead, I felt like he was mocking me. 'It's not some kind of joke,' I said uncomfortably. 'There are rules in the spirit world. Ghosts can't just go anywhere they want to.'

Squeezing my hand, he said, 'I know it's not a joke. Look, I'm not explaining very well. Let's start again.'

I studied him for a minute, then nodded. 'OK.'

His face split into a grin. 'Excellent. Did I tell you how much I missed you?'

'You didn't text me, though.'

Reaching into his blazer pocket, he waved his mobile at me. 'No signal in the mountains. Sorry.'

I could believe there wouldn't be much mobile coverage in the wilds of the hills. 'How much did you miss me?'

'Loads,' he replied. I thought he might kiss me but instead, he let go of my hand and looked around. 'Hey, we're almost at the cemetery. I've always wanted to take a look around. Up for it?'

Er, how about no? Graveyards weren't the hang-out of choice for good psychic girls like me. 'It's closing soon,' I objected.

He peered through the railings at an ivy-covered gravestone. 'Nah, I'm sure I read somewhere that it's open until five. Come on.'

I glanced at my watch. It was four o'clock and the sky was already darkening. I shook my head. 'I can't, Nico.'

He tugged on my hand. 'Of course you can. Unless you're scared?'

I was. Cemeteries were full of restless spirits and not all of them were friendly to the living. But the conversation was only just beginning; there was more I wanted to know and we could hardly talk freely in the juice bar. 'I don't want to —'

'Come on, Skye. Just a quick visit. In and out, I promise, and if we meet any ghosts, I'll scare them away.'

I let him pull me down the hill towards the entrance, trying to ignore my misgivings. The cemetery itself was split in two. The east cemetery was surrounded by iron fencing and open to the public on payment of a token fee towards upkeep of the ancient graves, but the west cemetery was enclosed in sturdy stone walls and kept securely locked. Jeremy had told me you could arrange a guided tour of the centuries-old tombs inside, but I'd shivered at the thought. Who knew what you might bump into?

We turned through the ornate wrought-iron gates into the east cemetery and I waited in silent anxiety as Nico paid for us to go in, glancing past the ticket office to the green-laced paths beyond.

'The gates close in an hour,' the woman in the kiosk said as she tore two tickets from the grey roll and slid them across the desk. 'Be back by quarter to five or you'll be here for the night.'

Nico winked at me and handed me one of the tickets. 'Don't worry about us, we're too chicken to get locked in,' he said.

Forcing down a bad feeling, I followed him into the cemetery. It would be OK, I told myself through gritted teeth. The ghosts who lived there would have better things to do than torment an innocent psychic. Wouldn't they?

'Did you know Karl Marx is buried here?' Nico turned to me, his eyes gleaming. 'Hey, maybe you'll see him. How cool would that be?'

'On a scale of one to ten?' I said, pretending to think about it. 'Minus fifty. I doubt he's still here, anyway. I told you, it's only ghosts with unfinished business who stick around.'

I shivered and wrapped my blazer more closely around myself. Dusk had brought a definite chill to the air and the long shadows made by the lamps weren't doing anything to set my mind at rest. A tall marble angel loomed over us on our left and a crumbling mausoleum leaned precariously to the right. 'Can we just see whatever it is you want to see and get out of here?' I asked. 'This place is seriously creeping me out.'

Nico raised an eyebrow. 'I'd have thought you'd be right at home here. Plenty of people to talk to.'

Something skittered past in the tangle of green on the edge of my vision. I turned my head sharply but there was nothing there. 'Let's just say that some ghosts don't like the living.'

His teeth flashed in the fading daylight. 'They're the most interesting ones.'

We arrived at a fork in the path. I glanced down one of the paths. It was brightly lit, but even so I wasn't especially keen on going down it. The other one was dim and shadowy and looked about as uninviting as it was possible to look. A damp, rotting scent filled the air, the smell of decaying vegetation and musty earth. Nico threw me a sideways glance and grabbed my hand. 'Ready to be spooked?'

Before I could answer, he broke into a run, dragging me behind him down the left-hand fork.

'No, Nico!' I tried to pull my hand from his, but he tightened his grip.

'Where's your spirit of adventure, Skye?' he called

over his shoulder, flashing me a wicked grin as he twisted down another fork. 'Ha ha – spirit. Get it?'

Oh great, now he was doing stand-up. I wasn't in the mood for jokes. In fact, the way I felt at the moment, as soon as he stopped hauling me along he was going to be getting an almighty thump. 'Stop,' I begged, twisting my fingers desperately.

I don't know whether he heard the panic in my voice, but he slowed down. 'You're right,' he said, his voice bouncing off the jagged and worn headstones lining the path. 'This place is seriously creepy. Have you seen any ghosts yet?'

My breath misted in the chilly air as I caught my breath. Willing my pounding heart to slow, I took refuge behind sarcasm. 'Oh yeah, that's Jim Morrison over there, having a smoke with Kurt Cobain.'

Nico grinned. 'Kurt Cobain was cremated and Jim Morrison is buried in Paris. What would they be doing here?'

A sound in the shadow-filled undergrowth behind us made me jump. 'Trying to find their way out, if they had any sense.' I turned pleading eyes on him. 'Please can we go now?'

He stared down at me, his eyes unreadable in the gloom. 'We're not leaving until we've found a ghost.'

'You're joking.' Even as I said it, I knew he wasn't. There was something about his expression that told me he'd planned this all along. With a chilled wrench of my stomach, I realised he'd never had any intention of going back to the gates before closing time. Whatever had happened in Romania had changed him.

He shook his head solemnly. 'No, Skye, I'm not joking.' He reached out to tuck a tendril of hair behind my ear. 'You're the most fascinating girl I've ever met. My dad's been teaching me about the paranormal for as long as I can remember, but it all comes so easily to you. You're a natural.'

'What do you mean, a natural?' I asked, even though I knew what he meant. Peering down at my watch, I struggled to make out the position of the hands.

'Naturally psychic,' he said. 'You don't need rituals like we do to speak to spirits.'

Who did he mean by we? 'Rituals?' I asked.

He nodded. 'Ancient binding spells to summon the dead. He wants to meet you, by the way,' Nico went on. 'But I'm not sharing you with anyone. Not yet.'

A shiver of uneasiness crawled over me. 'Take me home, Nico. I'll show you a ghost, if that's what you want.'

He threw me a disbelieving look. 'Whatever.'

'I mean it; my aunt's house is haunted. We don't have to hang out here.' I shivered fearfully and glanced around, searching for signs of movement among the tangle of ivy and marble. There had to be ghosts here;

it was only a matter of time before one found us.

'But not the kind I'm looking for.' His voice was harsh in the falling darkness. 'I want exactly the sort of ghost a good psychic like you tries to avoid.'

I shook my head. 'You don't know what you're talking about. This isn't a horror film you can switch off. The dead can be dangerous.'

'Not to me.' He smiled and I became even more certain that he'd changed during his trip away. The boy staring down at me now with eyes as cold as the blackest frozen lake was a different person to the one I'd fallen in love with. Dontay had been right; there was something very wrong. 'I haven't told you the best bit about my trip yet.'

I watched his breath cloud between us, the iciness in my bones deeper than the falling temperature merited. 'Oh?'

He looked up at the sky thoughtfully. 'The family friends I mentioned back in Romania? They're not exactly what you'd call friends.'

That must have been what he'd meant earlier, when he'd called them his clan, I decided. Dontay had been right about that, too. I didn't care any more what Nico wanted to tell me – I was frightened and wanted to go home. If I could distract him, I could make a run for it. 'Go on.'

'Ever heard of Dracula?'

In spite of my terrified state, I rolled my eyes. 'Oh, please. You don't seriously expect me to believe you're a vampire?'

His mouth curved into a smile. I resisted the temptation to check for suddenly pointy teeth. 'There's no such thing. But the legend of Vlad Dracul came out of the Carpathian Mountains. All sorts of stories come out of there, and not all of them are fairy tales.'

I hugged myself, rubbing my arms briskly as my gaze darted sideways into the shadows. 'Spare me the dramatic build-up and get to the point, Nico.'

He shrugged easily. 'Romanian legend tells of an ancient order called the Solomonarii, who used magic to do great good. The oldest tales say that Dracula himself was a member.'

I went still. 'Dracula's not exactly famous for his social work, is he?' I clamped my teeth together to stop my teeth from chattering. As if I wasn't cold enough, tendrils of fog were creeping towards us – just what I needed.

'There were nine members originally and they studied for years to master the skills to do their work. Skills like being able to control the weather, for example.' He glanced around contemplatively at the blanket of white mist snaking around our feet. 'Or the ability to talk to the dead and bend the spirit world to their will.'

I'd like to see anyone try to bend Mary Drover to do

their bidding. She'd bamboozle them with babble. I stared at Nico, trying to shake off the horrible feeling that he really had joined a gang, and not just any gang either – the kind that made the London Fields Posse look like a bunch of playschool kids. 'Why are you telling me this now?'

His black eyes sought mine. 'Come on, Skye, why do you think I'm telling you? What if I told you the stories aren't all make-believe? That the Solomonarii really exist?'

Trying to ignore the dense fog, I summoned up a disdainful look. 'So what if they do? What has that got to do with me?'

He grinned, but there was no trace of humour in it. 'Quite a lot, actually.' He took a step closer and I cowered at the undisguised menace in his tone. 'Because last week I finally became one of them. And you have something I need.'

Chapter 16

It was a joke; it had to be.

I backed away from him. 'That's not funny, Nico.'

'It's not meant to be. It is true, though.' He waved a hand at the whiteness surrounding us. It was waist high. 'I decided on fog, for added atmosphere, but I could produce a few lightning bolts if it'll help.'

'Stop it.'

He raised an eyebrow and a fork of brilliant white light split the darkness. I jumped violently and felt the colour drain from my face. My brain stuttered and refused to absorb what my senses were telling it. Nico couldn't be controlling the weather; it had to be a coincidence. But how likely was a lightning strike at the exact second he demanded one?

'All of the Solomonarii are born with a birthmark.'

He dragged the hair behind his left ear back. Involuntarily, I looked up and saw an ugly, puckered mark, dark against his pale skin. 'I think it looks like a mask. What do you think?'

The black mark was striking and I could see why he thought it looked like a mask. That explained why he kept his hair longer than the rest of the boys as well. I'd assumed he was working the rock god look but he'd actually been hiding something which would have caused awkward comments at school. I ignored his question. 'Loads of people have birthmarks. It doesn't mean they're members of a secret society.'

He sighed impatiently. 'Still not convinced? How about some thunder?'

On cue, a deep boom rumbled ominously overhead, and I couldn't deny the truth any more. I was suddenly more scared than I'd ever been. 'You're not joking.'

He clapped slowly. 'Well done.'

And if he was telling the truth about the weather, that must mean —

'Can you really talk to the dead?' I blurted out.

'Not yet,' he said. 'Controlling the weather is easy, but I can't seem to contact the spirit world. So that's why I need you.'

A shudder ran through me. Was this what Dontay had heard him say I wouldn't do? 'I'm not being your mouthpiece, if that's what you think.'

He eyed me, a look of genuine puzzlement on his face. 'We've got something good together. Why not make it better?'

I glared back at him. 'Well, let's see. You lie about why you wanted to come in here, drag me about like I'm a rag-doll and get me totally lost.' A horrible thought occurred to me. 'You planned this from the very beginning, didn't you?'

'What?' he said, surprised. 'Of course I didn't. Although you caught my interest much more than I expected.'

'Liar,' I said savagely. 'The gig at the Roundhouse was meant to make me fall head over heels for you, wasn't it, so I'd help you talk to ghosts? Well, here's a newsflash, Nico: you're not that irresistible.'

He looked away. 'You've got it all wrong,' he answered in a low voice. 'I had no idea there was anything unusual about you when I saw you in that alley with Peterson. You just seemed like you needed my help, and for some reason I wanted to protect you. Then I got to know you, and the more I found out, the more I wanted to know.'

'And you needed to trap me here so you could tell me that?'

He shook his head. 'New members of the Solomonarii have to pass an initiation test. They have to prove to the other members that they can influence a ghost for the good of the order.' Then his shoulders slumped in defeat. 'I hoped you'd be able to help.'

He looked so vulnerable that for a moment I was almost tempted. But then common sense kicked in. I didn't know why the Solomonarii were so obsessed with manipulating the dead, but their reasons couldn't be honourable. What I needed was to buy myself a bit of time to work out how to get away. I pursed my lips and pretended to think. 'Let's just say I help you. What do I have to do? And what happens to the ghost?'

'Once the order has evidence that I control the spirit, we let it go.'

There was a subtle shift behind his eyes and I knew it wasn't the truth. I wondered what kind of evidence the Solomonarii would need – how did you prove you could command a ghost? The ones I'd met had minds of their own and rarely did as they were told.

My own eyes strayed to the watch on my wrist; it was five minutes to closing time. If I had any chance of getting out of there before the gates were padlocked for the night, I had to go now and hope that the direction I chose led me back to the exit.

'It looks like you're in luck,' I said, pointing over his left shoulder. 'There's a ghost coming now.'

I didn't really expect it to work, but his eyes flickered backwards and he twisted around. Hoping my legs were long enough to find the target, I raised my knee as hard as I could. Nico's agonised groan told me I'd hit him exactly where I'd intended. As he doubled over and sank to the ground, I ran faster than I'd ever run before. The fog blocked out any trace of the lamplight and nothing looked the same as it had on the way in; I could only hope I was going in the right direction. I knew it wouldn't be long before Nico was following me, and a muffled pounding behind me told me he was already on my trail. I didn't think he'd actually hurt me, but there was no way I wanted to spend the night in Highgate Cemetery.

Something struck my face, bouncing off my cheek. The sharp pain caused my eyes to fill with tears and I gasped. Slowing, I swept both hands from the bridge of my nose across each cheek, wondering if I'd been bitten. Then I felt the stab of tiny needles on the top of my head and shoulders. I looked up. Shards of ice were falling from the sky. I held out a hand to catch a hailstone; it was the size of a marble. A second later, giant hail was tumbling around me. Throwing half a glance backwards, I sped up, ignoring the sickening crunch of snail shells under my feet. In a few minutes the hail would turn the path into an ice rink, not to mention cut my face to ribbons.

A roaring gust of wind nearly knocked me off my feet as I reached the point where the path had forked. Struggling to stay upright and ignoring the treacherous hailstones, I hurtled forwards, praying I'd reach the exit without breaking my neck. The wind did me a favour; up ahead, I caught a glimpse of a faint light through the flailing trees. It was too low to be one of the lamp-posts. My heart leaped. Maybe it was a torch.

'Wait!' I yelled and forced my legs to move faster. 'Wait for me!'

The shaft of light paused and swung towards me. 'Is there someone there?'

A ragged sob rose up in my throat. 'Yes! Please don't lock me in.'

I slowed as I got closer to the torch and relief flooded through me. Wrapped up in a fluorescent raincoat was the woman who'd sold us our tickets and she had a large bunch of keys in her hand. Her face glowed eerily inside the yellow hood. 'I thought everyone had left already. Come on, I'm just locking up. Terrible weather, isn't it?'

She turned away. I glanced uneasily over my shoulder. There was no sign of Nico and I didn't know what I'd do if he appeared on the path behind me. As we reached the heavy iron gates, I chewed at my lip. Should I tell the woman he was still inside?

The gate swung open and the woman gestured at me to leave. 'What an awful storm,' she said. Then she frowned. 'Weren't there two of you?'

A flurry of hail battered at my head, causing me to lift a soggy arm in protection as we were buffeted by the wind. A sudden burst of rage charged through me. I was chilled to the bone, shocked and soaking, all thanks to Nico. He'd shown no mercy when he'd tried to make me help him. Why should I show any to him?

'He left before me,' I said, crossing my fingers inside my sleeve and stepping through the gate. 'Thanks for letting me out.'

I walked away without looking back, determined not to give in to the tears I felt prickling behind my eyes. As I moved further away from the cemetery, the wind died down and the vicious hailstorm petered away to nothing. I guessed Nico could only control the weather in his immediate vicinity. I heard the heavy clang of gates behind me and tried to ignore the guilty whisper that I was abandoning him. There would be another way out, I was sure – maybe a gap in the fence alongside the neighbouring Waterlow Park, or he'd find a way over the wall – so he wouldn't be there all night. But hopefully by the time he got out, I'd be long gone. I shook my numbed head, stunned by the evening's events. What had happened to the real Nico; the one who'd taken me to the Roundhouse and made me forget everything when he kissed me? Was he trapped inside the monster I'd left in the cemetery? I choked back a sudden sob at the memory of his cruel expression and hurried home.

Chapter 17

Celestine knew there was something wrong the second I stumbled through the front door.

'Get out of those wet clothes and into the shower,' she commanded, as my bag fell from my icy fingers and thudded on to the floor. 'I'll make you a hot drink.'

By the time the warm water had chased the last of the chill from my bones and I had dragged myself reluctantly out of the shower, the cup of tea had gone stone cold. After wrapping me up on the sofa under a fleecy blanket, Celestine made another and then settled beside me.

'What happened? And don't say you got caught out in a downpour, I can see it was much more than that.'

Her blue eyes stared into mine and I knew there was no point in holding anything back. In a halting voice I told her everything. When I'd finished, she was silent.

'Do you think we should call someone, to let them know he's in there?' I asked.

She shook her head. 'He's got a mobile, right?' When I nodded, she went on, 'Then I doubt he's still there. He'd have called for help if he couldn't find a way out.'

Another worry rose up to take the place of the one she'd just put to rest. 'What if he did meet a ghost?'

There was a derisive snort from the doorway. I looked up to see Mary hovering there, and from the look on her face she'd heard everything.

'There art dark and restless souls in yonder grave-yard,' she said, grinning unpleasantly. 'Mayhap the young fool received his heart's desire and will bother thee no more.'

'Haven't you ever heard that it's rude to eavesdrop?' I demanded. As scared as I'd been in the cemetery, I wouldn't wish an evil spirit on anyone.

She raised a grime-covered hand to shake a warning finger at me. 'The Solomonarii mean harm to all in the ghostly realm. If one should fall before gaining full strength it would be a blessing.'

No matter what Nico had done, I didn't want any harm to come to him. 'Just who are the Solomonarii?' I asked Celestine, not at all sure I was ready for her answer. 'Dontay thought they might be a gang, but I couldn't find anything on Google. Have you ever heard of them?'

'Not for a long time,' she said, her voice troubled. 'And never outside of Romania. What did you say Nico's surname was again?'

'Albescu.'

'They are unholy men,' Mary intoned, determined to make us listen to her. 'They do the devil's shaded work.'

This seemed a bit rich, coming from a self-proclaimed witch who'd made it her mission to torment the life out of me. 'Gee, Mary, you think?'

Celestine looked worried. 'She's right. The Solomonarii might have started out pretending to work for the good of mankind, but it didn't take long for people to realise they were serving a darker master.'

'Who?' I asked, my imagination conjuring up a bizarre cross between Satan and the genie from Aladdin.

'No one knows. Their castle in Romania is called the Scholomance but the locals know it better as the Devil's Academy.'

'And they really communicate with the dead?'

Mary gave a hollow laugh. 'They seek to commune with us but care not if the act consumes us.'

I glanced at my aunt helplessly. 'Translation?'

Her expression grew serious. 'The Solomonarii don't just talk to the dead. They put the dead to work for them. By the time they've finished with them, the ghost is nothing more than an empty shell. They call them the Eaten. If Nico's father is a member, then that would explain why Nico has been sucked in.'

Her words filled me with horror. I didn't know what was worse: the thought of a ghost being used to do evil or the idea that Nico could be involved in something so terrible. 'What are we going to do?'

Celestine shook her head sadly. 'We can consult the other psychics at the Dearly D. They might have some suggestions. In the meantime, keep away from Nico in case his powers grow.'

I wasn't exactly filled with confidence. His powers had seemed pretty strong already. 'What do we do if he is controlling a spirit?'

Mary raised a dirt-encrusted finger and dragged it across her throat. I felt the colour drain from my face.

'Why don't we cross that bridge when we get to it?' Celestine cut in, offering me a reassuring smile. 'In the meantime, make sure you're not alone with him. Would it help if I spoke to your teachers?'

I stared at my folded hands, an empty feeling rising up inside me. I'd trusted Nico. Was it only a week ago that I'd been crying myself to sleep because I missed him so much? Now he'd betrayed me and I was scared to see him again. I shivered, remembering his face as he'd summoned the thunder and lightning. Whoever the Solomonarii were, they couldn't be a force for good if joining them brought about such a drastic change in someone's personality. What kind of monster forced his son into such a clan? Unless it had been Nico's choice and he'd been acting out a role when he'd been kissing me? Maybe he'd only pretended to care about me and the darkness was his true character. The thought made me want to throw up.

Aware that Celestine was waiting for an answer, I said, 'I don't think so.' I felt my voice crack. 'It's going home that worries me.'

Mary drifted towards us. 'Fear not. I shall guard thy steps at the rising of the sun and the fall of each night.'

She bared her blackened teeth in a stumpy smile and my heart rose a little bit more. As minders went, I could do a lot worse than Mary. If Nico so much as flicked a snowflake in my direction, he'd have Mary to deal with. The smallest of smiles tugged at my mouth at the thought. She might not have the presence of a prize-winning boxer, but she knew how to fight dirty. I had no doubt who would come off worst.

Mary was as good as her word. Every morning after that, she accompanied me to the school gates and she was waiting there for me at the end of the day. I could only guess how many of the other kids walked through her as she stood watching me cross the playground. From the pained expression on her face it was more than one, and I felt bad that I'd ever wished she didn't exist.

I'd decided not to tell Dontay about my encounter in

the cemetery. He thought little enough of Nico as it was; it was better to pretend we'd split up. Besides, he seemed constantly on edge these days; Nelson was getting in deeper with Shank and had started lying to his parents about where he was going and who with. Dontay had enough on his plate without me adding to it. Anyway, given the amount of pent-up anger I felt rolling off him every time I saw him recently, I couldn't be sure he wouldn't go and teach Nico the kind of lesson he'd never forget. The last thing I needed was a ghost with a taste for blood.

It hurt to see Nico every day without ever knowing if he'd really cared about me. In some ways I preferred not knowing; the thought that the real Nico was trapped somewhere inside that monstrous side he'd shown at the cemetery kept me awake at nights. But as long as we each pretended the other didn't exist things were mostly bearable. The official line was that we'd split up after a massive argument. Megan refused to believe it but she could see how much I was hurting and morphed into a kind of weird, overprotective guardian angel. If anyone so much as looked at me the wrong way she bit their head off; the other kids started crossing the corridor to avoid us, including Ellie, and I'm sure even some of the teachers were scared of her.

It helped that Nico himself was avoiding me like I was a plague victim; I'd seen him ducking into corridors to escape me. Knowing that he wanted nothing to do with me gave our relationship a sense of finality. I tried to ignore the heaviness of my heart and told myself it was the only way to get him out of my system.

Given Megan's concern, I guess I shouldn't have been surprised that she caught my hastily swallowed gasp when Dontay materialised through the wall of our Tuesday morning English lesson the following week.

'Are you OK?' she whispered, leaning closer. 'You look like you've seen a ghost.'

Thankfully, she had no idea how right she was. My hands had gone clammy and my heart hammered in my ears. After our last meeting at school, there was only one reason he'd come to find me there: Nelson was in trouble.

'I feel a bit sick,' I whispered back, and it was only half a lie. Dontay's eyes scanned the class until he saw me in the second-to-back row.

'Finally,' he said. 'I've been everywhere. You had to be in the last room I went to, didn't you?'

I stared at him wordlessly, hoping he'd remember I couldn't answer him.

'Make an excuse and get out of here.' Dontay's voice was flat but I caught his underlying panic. 'Nelson bunked off school today and no one knows where he is, except me.' A flash of urgency sparked from his eyes. 'Something's going down. He's got a gun.'

The classroom spun crazily before my eyes. I gripped the table in front of me and tried to ignore the terror bubbling up inside me.

Megan frowned in concern and pressed a cool hand against my cheek. 'You look awful.'

I turned to her. 'I have to go.'

Her frown deepened. 'Yeah, sure. I'll come with you.'

'No!' I got to my feet and took a deep breath. Now the rest of the class was watching me, as well as Megan. 'I don't feel well, miss. Can I go to the toilet, please?'

Mrs Craig lowered her copy of *The Crucible* and peered at me. 'You are very pale.' Her scarlet lips pursed and she sighed. 'Go on, then. Don't be long.'

Megan's worried gaze followed me all the way to the door. I'd have to drop her a text to let her know I wouldn't be back that day. As I staggered out into corridor and let the door close behind me, I couldn't help thinking that if things were as bad as Dontay feared, there was a chance I might not be back at all.

Chapter 18

'We should go to the police,' I told Dontay as soon as we were clear of the school buildings. Dontay was hell-bent on getting out of school as quickly as possible and, since I didn't have the luxury of walking through walls, I had to run along the corridors to catch up with him outside. It was lucky the halls were quiet and I didn't have to explain myself to anyone, although Dr Bailey spotted us through the window and I cringed as his angry shouts followed us across the playground. I was relieved we didn't bump into Nico either; the last thing I needed in my stressed state was an encounter with him.

'Why?' Dontay fired back at me. 'You said they never listened to Jeremy when he tried to talk to them. What makes you think they'll listen to you?'

'That's because I told him not to give them Nelson's

name, so he wouldn't get into trouble,' I said. 'And look where that got us. We have to trust them. I can't do this on my own.'

'No coppers,' Dontay replied in a flat voice. 'Involving them only makes people shoot first and ask questions later. Anyway, you've got me.'

But he won't be much help if bullets start flying around, a voice whispered in my brain. I thought hard and reached into my blazer. 'Let me at least text Celestine. Or Jeremy,' I said, flipping the handset open. 'Maybe they can talk to someone at Scotland Yard and —'

Dontay stopped in his tracks and knocked the phone out of my hand. 'No! They'll try to stop you going.'

Rubbing my stinging fingers, I knelt down and started to pick up the scattered pieces of my phone. 'So what exactly do you want me to do? Because Nelson isn't going to listen to a word I say, remember?'

He took a deep breath and ran his fingers through his close-cropped hair. 'There's some stuff I haven't told you. When I realised how tight Nelson was with the gang, I started following some of the other gang members, listening in on their chats with Shank.'

The tingle in my fingers was subsiding, but anxiety was making me clumsy. I fumbled with the shards of plastic, trying to clip them together. Then I saw that I was fighting a losing battle. The clips were broken. 'And?'

'I know what the plan is. There's this guy called Tyrone in the Marsh Street Massive who's been disrespecting Shank big time. He's been saying how Shank isn't a proper gang leader and that the London Fields Posse will never be the top gang in Hackney.'

My hands drifted to my sides, my damaged phone momentarily forgotten. 'I bet that hasn't gone down well with Shank.'

He sneered derisively. 'Yeah, you got that right. So Shank wants to shut Tyrone up. And he's going to use my brother to do it.'

I stared at him. 'You mean Nelson has to – hurt Tyrone?'

Dontay's nod was grim. 'Last night, he told Nelson that the bullet which killed me came from Tyrone's gun.' He swallowed and looked away. 'Shank said he heard Tyrone laughing about how I'd cried for my mum when I died. And then Shank told Nelson to go to the scrap metal merchants down by the railway arches and collect a package. He said Tyrone would be down the snooker hall this afternoon and Nelson could see how much he cried when he bled to death.'

A shudder ran through me at the thought of Dontay in pain and afraid. He was ashamed of crying, I realised, but he had nothing to be embarrassed about. If it had been me who'd been shot, I'd have screamed until my breath was gone. 'Do you think he'll go through with it?'

He shrugged brokenly. 'He picked up the package this morning.'

I didn't need Dontay to confirm what had been inside. 'So Nelson has a gun,' I said in a flat voice, the blood turning glacial in my veins. 'Can't we go to your parents?'

'And say what? My mum would freak out and my dad would storm over there and get himself shot.'

'So what are we going to do?'

His face was a mask of determined misery. 'We have to stop him, Skye. Either he's going to shoot Tyrone or he's going to get himself killed. One way or another, his life will be over. I can't let that happen.'

I glanced at my watch. It was half past eleven. We only had a few hours to get across London and stop Nelson becoming another street-crime statistic. Whether we'd make it was anyone's guess.

If you've ever tried to get from Highgate to Hackney, you'll know it's a nightmare. It's not far if you've got wings, but they were in short supply, and travelling by public transport in the London traffic seemed to take forever. It was a thousand times worse because I didn't have my earpierce and so couldn't talk openly to Dontay while we were on the bus or the train. I was also conscious of the suspicious looks my school uniform was getting – I might as well have had a flashing neon *truant* sign over my head. By the time we made it to Homerton station, Dontay seemed ready to burst with pent-up frustration, and I knew exactly how he felt. If we stood any chance of stopping Nelson from doing the unimaginable we needed to catch him before he reached the snooker hall and then find a way to get through to him. But neither of us had the first clue where to start and it was already nearly one o'clock.

'Maybe we should head straight to the snooker hall,' I said. 'We know he'll turn up there eventually.'

Dontay nodded and looked me up and down. 'We should get you off the street. There's a greasy spoon opposite you can watch from. You won't stand out so much then.'

We walked silently from the station to the high street, each of us deep in our own heads. From the moment I'd agreed to help Dontay find Nelson, I'd put myself in danger and I knew Celestine would go mental if she knew. I didn't see what else I could do, though. If I refused to help then I'd be condemning not only Nelson but Dontay as well, because how could Dontay move on if his brother was dead?

The snooker hall was sandwiched between a pound shop and a cheap-looking hairdresser's. The name O'Sullivan's was picked out on a faded green canopy above the grimy doorway and I guessed the hall itself must be on the first floor. Just as Dontay had said, there was a café directly opposite and we headed inside. It wasn't the classiest place I'd ever been, but it was warm and there was an empty table in the window. I'd barely had time to settle into the hard plastic seat and sip my industrial-strength tea before Dontay raised his arm and pointed across the street.

'That's Tyrone. He's the one smoking.'

There were three men standing outside the snooker hall. They were older than Dontay – I guessed they must be around twenty. Tyrone was in the middle, a baseball cap pulled low over his eyes. The other two seemed to be having some kind of argument, but Tyrone wasn't paying attention. His gaze flicked up and down the street as he dragged on his cigarette. Then he flicked the butt on to the pavement and jerked his head towards the entrance. The three of them tapped fists and Tyrone disappeared inside, leaving his mates to walk off down the street.

My insides cramped with anxiety. If what Dontay had told me was true, these were dangerous men. What could I possibly hope to achieve on my own?

'There's still time to go to the police,' I whispered.

Dontay shook his head in scorn. 'They'll arrest Nelson straight off, and no decent football club will touch him if he's got a criminal record before they even sign him.'

He stood even less chance if he was wounded or

dead, I wanted to point out, but I kept the thought to myself. Instead, I shifted uncomfortably in my seat and met his gaze. 'I'm scared, Dontay.'

His shoulders slumped and his expression became pleading. 'Listen, all you got to do is talk him out of going in there. Then you can call whoever you want.'

I opened my mouth to argue, then saw the workmen at the table next to me casting sneaky glances my way and closed it again. The last thing I needed was to attract more suspicion. I'd have to put my trust in Dontay and try to forget what had happened the last time I'd trusted someone.

Slouched down in my seat, I made my tea last as long as I could, but it was soon down to the dregs and there was no sign of Nelson. I reached into my pocket and counted up the coins there; I had enough for one more cup. After that I'd have to find somewhere else for my surveillance. In other circumstances I might have felt a tiny thrill at playing James Bond, but there was too much at stake – people's lives for one thing, and quite possibly my own.

I got to my feet to go to the counter and order more tea but Dontay stopped me. 'He's here.'

I peered out of the window. Nelson was walking slowly along the other side of the road, head down and eyes fixed on the pavement. Snatching my bag from under the table, I threaded my way to the door and stepped out into the cold.

'Nelson!' I yelled, hoping my voice would carry over the traffic. 'Wait!'

He looked around when he heard his name but didn't stop. Dontay was across the road in a flash; he didn't have cars and motorbikes to worry about. Fretfully, I waited for a bus to trundle past before picking my way to the other side. Nelson had almost reached the entrance to O'Sullivan's. I hitched up my bag and ran towards him.

'Nelson, I need to talk to you,' I called, my voice wobbling as my feet pounded the pavement. 'It's really important!'

He flicked a dismissive hand at me and kept walking. 'Save it, yeah? I ain't listening.'

I threw a despairing glance at Dontay. Now what?

'Tell him you know about the gun.' Dontay's eyes were focused on his brother. 'Tell him you'll go to the police.'

Heart pounding, I dug my fingernails into my palms. 'You've got a gun,' I blurted. 'The police would be interested to know that.'

Nelson stopped with one hand on the door handle of the snooker hall. He turned slowly and stared at me. 'Who told you about that?'

I swallowed and raised my chin. 'The way I heard it, Shank has you doing his dirty work. Do you think that's what your brother would have wanted?'

Nelson stepped closer. 'You said that last time. Who

do you think you are, deciding what he wanted?'

'I told you, I was a friend of Dontay's. He wouldn't want you to do anything stupid.'

Instantly, I knew I'd said the wrong thing. Nelson's expression became sneering. 'I think it ain't nothing to do with you. So why don't you go home, before someone does something stupid to you.'

Before I could respond, he yanked the door of the club open and barged through. It swung closed behind him.

'Follow him,' Dontay commanded, agitation colouring his voice. 'You have to stop him.'

I peered through the grime-covered entrance. 'How? I'm not old enough to get in.'

'They shouldn't let Nelson in either, but they will,' Dontay said and walked though the door.

Alone on the street, I stared after him and went through my options. Either I could find the nearest policeman and spill the whole story to him, or I could follow Dontay inside and try one more time to talk Nelson out of doing something he'd regret for the rest of his life, however long that was. Going to the police was the easiest option, but would they react in time? If only my phone wasn't broken. I pictured Nelson walking up the stairs right now, drawing his gun as he went. Would he threaten Tyrone first or would he just shoot? What if Tyrone was armed as well, or one of his mates? The gunfight would be over before the police even knew about it, let alone stop it. I blinked back tears, chewing my lip anxiously. Deep down I knew I didn't really have a choice; I was going inside. I had to do everything I could to stop the madness that was about to unfold. The last time I'd squared up to bullies, Nico had saved me. I doubted anyone would come to my rescue this time.

Chapter 19

The interior of the snooker hall was dark, in spite of the cheap fluorescent lights flickering above our heads. I blinked, letting my eyes adjust to the gloom. As I'd guessed, entry to the snooker hall itself was up a staircase behind a cash desk and a solid-looking turnstile. An overweight, bald man in a grubby shirt sat behind the glass screen, watching me suspiciously. There was no sign of Dontay.

Deciding I'd brazen it out, I folded my arms over my blazer pocket with its conspicuous Heath Park badge and walked towards the desk. 'I'm a mate of Nelson's. All right if I go up?'

The man jerked a thumb at a notice on the wall behind him. 'Can't you read? No ID, no entry.'

I scowled. 'I bet you didn't ask Nelson for ID.'

An unpleasant smirk crossed the man's face. 'He don't need it. You do.'

It reminded me of the ID Nico had made for me at the Roundhouse. I pushed the memory away and scanned the stairs beyond the turnstile. Even if I'd had Megan's high-jump skills I'd have had no chance of clearing the barrier. Seeming to read my mind, the man tapped a baseball bat on the desk in front of him. 'Don't even think about it.'

Tears of defeat prickled my eyes and I turned away. I had no alternative now but to go to the police. Then Dontay appeared on the stairs and walked through the turnstile.

'I've been looking around. There's a fire escape around the back. Head to the alleyway, the door's open a bit.'

The rear of O'Sullivan's was even more sordid than the front. Rubbish was strewn along the dingy alley and dilapidated boxes were piled up against the walls. I picked my way along it, trying to work out which door-way would lead to the snooker hall. Something skittered near my feet. I shuddered and tried not to wonder what it had been. I'd heard that Londoners were never more than two metres from a rat – I didn't want to think about how much closer I'd just been.

In front, a door edged open and Dontay's head peered through it, lit by a faint glow. 'Hurry up.'

Slipping through the gap, I found myself blinking in the gloomy half-light again. 'I can't see a thing.'

'There's no bulb in the socket. You'll have to feel your way.'

He led, his faint glow barely visible in the dark. Gingerly, I shuffled forwards, hoping none of the rats from the alleyway had found their way inside. Reaching the bottom of a staircase, I gripped a slimy metal handrail and climbed upwards. I made out a sliver of light at the top; the way into the club. Dontay pushed the door back, his face a mask of grim concentration.

'All clear,' he called.

I pushed the door open further and eased my way past it. My nose wrinkled as the pungent smell of urine hit my nostrils and I glanced up to see I was standing beside the toilets. 'Where now?'

'Here.' Dontay headed through another door. Swallowing my fear, I eased the door back and followed, wondering what I'd find on the other side.

There were ten snooker tables in the hall, each gleaming emerald green under a pool of light coming from lamps above them. The rest of the hall was shrouded in darkness, except for a deserted bar which ran the length of one wall. Only one of the tables was in use, its brightly coloured balls like a handful of gems scattered randomly across the greenness. No one was playing on it now; the action was taking place nearby.

Framed by the light from the table, I made out Tyrone. He hadn't noticed me come in – his attention was focused on someone I couldn't see, stood beyond the reach of the light. But I didn't need to see to know it had to be Nelson. Just like I knew from Tyrone's tense expression that he had a gun pointed at him. My shoulders crumpled and I let out a silent, miserable breath; I was too late.

Keeping to the shadows, I edged closer until I had a clear view, and crouched behind one of the unused tables. Nelson's shoulders were hunched and he held his arm at a stiff right-angle to his body. The hand holding the gun barely trembled – I'd have been quivering like a jellyfish if it had been me. Dontay stood at his brother's shoulder, his face an agony of tension and sadness.

'Why?' Nelson said. 'Before I shoot you like you shot my brother, I want you to tell me why you killed him.'

Tyrone shrugged. 'I told you, man. I never done it,' he said, quiet insistence colouring his tone. 'I got no beef with you – I weren't even there the day it went down.'

Nelson threw him a sneering look. 'Shank told me you was. He said you wanted to show the London Fields Posse you meant business.'

Spreading his empty hands, Tyrone's gaze was intent. 'Then he's lying to you. And I'd want to know why if I was you.'

'What's that supposed to mean?'

'Why do you reckon Shank told you I shot Dontay? Maybe so you don't start asking too many questions about whose gun did the actual killing?'

I felt the tiny stab of pins and needles start to work their way along my legs and shifted as much as I dared behind the table. From the look on Dontay's face, he was mulling over Tyrone's words and I could see the dawn of doubt on his face. Nelson, though, was unconvinced.

'If you were a man, you'd take responsibility for what you done,' he said, his chin jutting out angrily. 'I should shoot you right now for being a coward.'

Deep in thought, Dontay didn't seem to hear his brother. 'I didn't see Tyrone there that day,' he said. The words were slow and heavy. His gaze was clouded with memories as realisation of the truth dawned. 'Shank was standing over me, talking on his phone, and I always thought he called the ambulance, but it was all so confusing. Maybe that's not how it went down.' He shook his head, as though trying to clear it. 'How could Tyrone have shot me if he wasn't even there?'

I saw my chance and seized it. 'Tyrone wasn't there, Nelson,' I called, standing up unsteadily on cramped legs and grateful for the support of the snooker table. 'But Shank was. Dontay saw him.'

Nelson swung towards me and I saw the flash of light on metal. 'You can't know that.'

His voice resonated with tension and I sensed he might snap at any second. Was there anything I could say to convince him to put the gun down? I licked my lips nervously and took the plunge. 'I can. He just told me.'

All of them swung towards me.

'What are you, some kind of nutter?' Nelson waved the gun at me, his face disbelieving. 'Just shut up, all right?'

The main door slammed back and a tall, skinny man stepped forwards. The light glinted off the heavy gold chains around his neck and he held a gun in his outstretched hand. He took in the scene with a disbelieving sneer. 'What is this, *The Jeremy Kyle Show*?'

Nelson froze. 'All right, Shank? I didn't know you were coming down here.'

Shank smiled and a mouthful of gold teeth glittered. 'I came to see how you got on with that little job I gave you, but I see it's taking longer than I expected.'

Tyrone watched him approach, a wary expression on his face. 'Sending a boy to do a man's job, Shank? What's the matter, you lost the stomach for killing these days?'

Shank let the smile drop. 'Finish the job,' he instructed Nelson.

Nelson's eyes were skittering nervously between Tyrone and Shank. 'He says he didn't do it.'

'Of course he does,' Shank said, his features twisting into a sadistic smirk. 'But you're gonna shoot him anyway, because I'm telling you to.'

Dontay was staring at Shank, a look of horror on his face. 'I remember. You were laughing on the phone as I lay there bleeding. You said you were the baddest gunman cos you'd got more bodies than anyone else.'

Shank was aiming his gun at Nelson now. 'And if you don't do it, I'll shoot you.' He gave a little gurgling laugh. 'Or maybe I'll shoot you anyway and blame it on Tyrone, like I did with your brother.'

Nelson twisted towards Shank, his face slack with shock. The hand with the gun dropped to his side. 'You?'

'Dontay weren't no loss.' Shank shrugged dismissively. 'His mind was always on football so when he got in the way during a battle with the Marsh Streeters, I saw a way to stir things up. There's nothing like a murder to fire the temper.'

Tears began to pour down Nelson's face. 'You?' he repeated. 'But I trusted you.'

Shank raised his gun higher and I saw his finger begin to tighten on the trigger. 'Yeah,' he said. 'You put your faith in the wrong person.'

It seemed as though time ground to a halt. I opened my mouth to scream, but no sound came out. Dontay launched himself at Shank and slid right through him. Tyrone was reaching beneath the snooker table for something I couldn't see. Shank squeezed the trigger of the gun. A single shot rang out, followed by a dull thud. My voice returned and I screamed, realising it was Shank who'd fired and knowing he couldn't have missed Nelson at such close range. But I was wrong. Instead of Nelson crumpling to his knees, it was Shank clutching at his leg and moaning, his gun clattering to the floor by his foot. Tyrone was the one who'd fired. Shank collapsed in a heap and I saw a lake of redness seeping from underneath his fingers. His gun tumbled next to him. The breath caught in my throat as Tyrone turned to aim at Nelson.

'Police, Nelson. Drop the gun!' he said.

Stunned, Nelson stared at the prone figure of Shank. The weapon fell from his fingers. Tyrone stepped forwards and kicked it away. It skittered under the table. 'Hands on the table where I can see them.' His gaze flickered towards me. 'You too.'

And then the hall rang with shouting voices as uniformed police officers poured through the door. In a daze, I watched as some bent over Shank and others frisked Nelson. The awful reality dawned on me when I caught the gleam of handcuffs clasped around his wrists. We were being arrested.

A female officer approached me, her face wary. 'Hands where I can see them, now!'

I stared at the floor as she checked me for weapons and clipped handcuffs on to me. Now that I knew we were out of immediate danger another kind of fear was crawling through me. Celestine might have got me involved with Dontay in the first place, but she could never have imagined how it would turn out. How on earth was I going to explain a trip to the police station?

Chapter 20

They kept us at Hackney police station for hours.
Celestine arrived, tight-lipped and grey-faced, and sat
with me through the interview. I didn't see Dontay at
all. Eventually, the police accepted my story that
although I knew Nelson, I had nothing to do with the
gangs; I'd simply been in the wrong place at the wrong
time. Tyrone, real name DS Hudson, had been part of a
deep undercover set-up called Operation Scorpion
designed to infiltrate gang culture in Hackney. He'd
known Shank was responsible for Dontay's murder but
needed proof. When he'd heard that the gang leader
was planning another murder, he'd agreed to be fitted
with a wire and a bulletproof vest. DS Hudson had
been ready to act as soon as Shank had admitted killing
Dontay, but had been forced to shoot him in the leg

when he'd threatened Nelson. I almost fainted with relief when they told me I was being released without charge. With stern warnings to keep out of trouble in future ringing in my ears, I followed Celestine out of the interview room and into the front of the police station.

Jeremy was sitting in the waiting area, staring straight ahead and trying not to make eye contact with anyone. He rose as the desk sergeant waved us through, but didn't speak until we were on the street outside the police station.

'All right?' he said, looking me up and down with concern.

It was the last straw. All the fear and stress of the day cracked my fragile self-control and I burst into tears.

'I'm so sorry,' I wailed, blinking at their serious expressions through sodden eyes. 'Dontay said Nelson had a gun and was going to shoot someone and he was so worried. I didn't know what to do and then it all went wrong.'

Celestine's face crumpled too and she wrapped me in a hug. 'You're safe. That's all that matters.'

'Please don't tell my mum!'

'Of course not,' Celestine murmured into my hair, clutching me tighter, and I trusted her. I stayed in her arms until the tears slowed, and then moved back.

Jeremy slipped an arm around my shoulders. 'You should have called us.'

My head drooped. 'I know. But everything happened so fast and my mobile got broken.'

'You've had a rough few weeks, but it's all over now.' Patting my arm sympathetically, he stepped back. 'Why don't I go and get the car?'

'Where's Dontay now?' Celestine asked as Jeremy headed towards the car park.

It was a good question. There was still no sign of him. Nelson had been taken into custody and I had no idea how that would affect his future. The detective questioning me had warned that possession of a firearm was a crime that carried a five-year jail sentence and that even a minor like Nelson could be sent to a young offenders' unit. Would Dontay be able to pass across to the astral plane with his brother's life in tatters? I didn't think so.

A cry rang out from the top of the police station steps. 'Skye!'

It was Dontay, and he was standing shoulder to shoulder with Nelson. Beside them was a stocky man and plump woman I guessed to be their parents. Dontay walked down the steps towards me.

'They've released him without charge,' he said when he reached us, jerking his head towards his brother.

My mouth dropped open in delighted surprise. 'That's great news. But what about the gun?'

Dontay grinned. 'He ditched it before he got to the

snooker hall.' Glancing back over his shoulder, his smile widened. 'The one we saw him carrying was a toy replica from home. He told the coppers he only wanted to scare Tyrone into admitting he'd killed me, he didn't want to shoot anyone.'

Celestine shook her head, blinking in disbelief. 'And it was Shank all along. How do you feel? Did you have any idea Shank was the one who caused your death?'

Dontay watched his family as they started to make their way down the steps, his expression reflective. 'No. I thought knowing who killed me would make a difference, but it doesn't, as long as Nelson is all right. And I doubt he'll be getting into trouble again any-time soon. He's grounded for the rest of his life.'

A shrill voice, with more than a hint of the West Indies about it carried towards us. 'I can't believe you worried us like that,' Mrs Ambrose was saying, one finger poking Nelson in the chest. Then she enveloped him in a crushing hug. 'After all we've been through with your poor brother, how could you risk your life getting involved with a gang? You're all we have now.'

Nelson let her hug him. He kept his gaze fixed on the ground and didn't look my way as they passed us by. 'I'm sorry, Mum.'

'And I don't suppose you thought about your future either. After we got that nice letter from the Youth Academy and everything.'

Nelson stopped and stared at his mother. 'What letter?'

Mrs Ambrose sniffed. 'They wanted you to go and try out for them, like Dontay did, but I don't suppose they'll be interested in someone with a criminal record.'

'Nelson hasn't got a record,' Mr Ambrose reminded his wife. 'He made a mistake is all.'

A dazed smile crept across Nelson's face. 'West Ham Youth Academy wants me to go for a trial?'

Mr Ambrose nodded. 'Next month. If we let you go.'

The conversation drifted away as they moved along the pavement. I had no doubt Nelson would be allowed to go to the trial, just as I knew West Ham would be mad not to sign him. The last bit of tension left me as I realised we'd succeeded. Nelson was going to be all right.

Next to me, Dontay arrived at the same conclusion. He punched the air in triumph. 'Yes!'

A faint twinkle as he made the gesture caught my eye. An incredulous frown crept across my forehead and I peered at him intently. 'Dontay, are you wearing glitter?'

Both Celestine and Jeremy turned to study him. Then my aunt broke into a gentle smile. 'So that's why you stayed, to make sure Nelson got what he really wanted.'

Dontay stared at her, confused. 'But I never done nothing.'

Celestine tilted her head. 'You introduced Skye to Nelson so that she could talk to him. If it hadn't been for you, he'd probably be badly injured right now, or even dead. One way or another, his dreams would be over. You stopped that from happening.'

I was so distracted by the sparkling lights settling around Dontay that I was barely listening to Celestine.

'What's happening?' I asked, bathing my fingers in the edge of his golden glow. 'Where are all these lights coming from?'

She took my hand and drew it gently away from Dontay. 'He's passing across.'

Dontay raised his own fingers and gazed at them in wonder. 'I'm what?'

My aunt smiled. 'Your time here is over,' she said, her voice soft with compassion. 'You've resolved the only thing holding you here and you're ready to start the next part of your journey.'

I saw a momentary flash of panic cross Dontay's face and he glanced around wildly for his family. 'But I didn't say goodbye.'

'You'll see them again one day. But if there's anything you want us to tell them for you, now would be a good time to say so.'

He gazed wistfully after his brother. 'I wish I'd told him how proud I was of him.'

Now that I knew Dontay was leaving, I realised how much I was going to miss him. We'd come a long way since our first awkward meeting at the Dearly D, and I could honestly say I'd never had a friend quite like him. My eyes filled up at the thought of the gap he was going to leave in my life. 'I'll make sure he knows.'

'And I never told my parents I love them.' His voice was growing fainter and I noticed with a jolt that I could see the lamp-post through him.

I swallowed, trying to shift the lump of emotion in my throat. 'I can tell them that too.'

He stared after them for a moment, before his face split into a beaming smile. 'Then I'm ready.' As he turned to me, I saw gratitude shining in his eyes. 'Thanks for everything, yeah? I know it wasn't easy.'

I couldn't hold back the tears any longer. 'That's OK. I – I hope they have football where you're going.'

Only his outline was visible now, picked out in tiny sparkling lights. He raised his fist to me in a final salute. 'Safe,' he said, and his voice was little more than a sigh. 'Sorry things didn't work out with Nico, Skye. Don't forget the offside rule.'

I gulped and smiled in spite of the tears. It was the first time he'd got Nico's name right. I'd never told him how Nico had betrayed me; I wondered what he'd call him if he knew the truth. 'Bye, Dontay.'

I thought I caught the faintest whispered goodbye, but I couldn't be sure. The last of the glow faded and Celestine and I were alone.

'He's gone,' I said brokenly. 'He's really gone.'

Celestine wrapped an arm around my shoulder. 'But he's at peace, and it's all thanks to you. You did a good job helping him.'

Sniffing and wiping my cheeks, I nodded. 'I'm going to miss him.'

The drama of the day was catching up with me and I was suddenly exhausted. I glanced along the road, hoping Jeremy was nearby with the car. As though he'd heard my silent prayer, he drew up to the kerb and leaned towards the open window. 'Get in. There's a traffic warden coming and I bet he'd love to give me a ticket.'

I rolled my eyes. After the day I'd had the last thing on my mind was a measly parking ticket. But Jeremy was twitching and I supposed I owed him for coming down to get me, so I swallowed my sigh and let my aunt lead me towards the car.

She squeezed my shoulders as we stood at the car door. 'Of course you'll miss him, but don't forget there are plenty more ghosts who need help. Like Isobel.'

Guilt wriggled through me. I'd left her to Jeremy and she was even following him to work. Deep down, I knew I'd been avoiding thinking about her, because I didn't know where to begin. 'She's not interested in me.'

Celestine tilted her head. 'She'll be a challenge, then. Make her interested.'

Her words made me feel small. Helping Dontay

had made me realise I liked making a difference to the spirits around me. All my life I'd wondered what my gift was for and now I knew I'd found my purpose. It was a good feeling. I wanted more.

My aunt was still talking. '. . . and I cleared it with Father Montgomery. You'd be working mostly with me but what do you think? The Dearly D could use another psychic on the staff, and perhaps you could take the heat off Jeremy with Isobel, before Mary unleashes the seven spirits of hell.'

'Do they even exist?' Then I blinked in astonishment as my brain caught up. 'Wait – are you offering me a job?'

A wry smile tugged at her lips as she pulled open the passenger door and got in. 'Why don't we call it an apprenticeship?'

I thought about that as I climbed into the car. My life had become bumpier than the fairground dodgems since I'd moved in with Celestine. I'd learned a lot in that short time – who I was, who I could trust and what a broken heart felt like. I could have done without that last one, to be honest, and wondered if Nico had any idea how much he'd hurt me. Megan didn't pretend to understand what had gone wrong between us but, like a true friend, she respected my right to privacy. Which reminded me, I'd never got the chance to text her after I'd left the school. She'd probably wasted all her credit texting me – I resolved to call her as soon as I got home.

I gazed from the back of my aunt's head to Jeremy's, thinking how great they'd been, especially in agreeing not to mention anything to my mum. They'd gone out of their way to help me settle into life without her. The least I could do was return the favour by getting Isobel over her crush on Jeremy. Actually, I quite fancied myself as a celestial matchmaker; maybe her Mr Right was out there in the spirit world, waiting to be found. He might even be a member of the Dearly D.

'A psychic apprenticeship?' I mused, settling back into the seat with a satisfied grin. 'I like the sound of that. Do you think we can stop at Hornsey Lane Bridge on the way home?' Jeremy's panic-filled eyes locked on me in the rear-view mirror. My grin widened. 'Relax, Romeo, you can drop me off round the corner. It's time someone told Isobel that today is the first day of the rest of her afterlife.'

Acknowledgements

Writing a book might seem like a one person job but in my case that isn't true. These are the people I owe big time:

Lee, for encouraging me, feeding me and putting up with my diva tendencies. You are still my favourite husband.

Tania, for being amazing and inspiring and sarcastic (if occasionally grumpy) and for reminding me what it's like to be a teenager. Thanks for being you.

My dad, Phil, who encouraged the teenage me to read. Thank you.

My in-laws, Richard and Janice, for always being so supportive and persuading everyone you know to buy my books.

Clare and Mike Watson, for lending me the northern Watson Writer's Retreat. The Woo-woos are on me.

Jo Williamson at Antony Harwood Ltd, agent extra-ordinaire and roller-coaster buddy – thanks for all the thrills so far, here's hoping the ride never ends.

Brenda, Ruth, Melissa, Vivien and the whole team

at Piccadilly Press, who spotted the promise of Skye and encourage me to get to know her. Thanks for being brilliant.

And lastly, thank you to anyone who read *My So-Called Afterlife* and took the time to tell me so. Keep those comments coming!

Find out what happens next for Skye and Nico . . .

My So-Called Phantom Lovelife

TAMSYN MURRAY

When fourteen-year-old Skye Thackery meets
Owen Wicks, it's not exactly love at first sight. She's
getting over a broken heart and he's, well, a ghost.

But as Sky gets to know him, she can't help wondering
what it would be like to kiss him. Dating a ghost isn't
easy, and things get worse when Owen declares he's
found a way to stay with Skye forever. His plans
make her uneasy – the shadowy organisation
which claims to be able to help him is bad news,
and it seems Nico, her ex, is involved too.

As Owen prepares to risk everything, Skye begins
to wonder if she really has a future with him,
or if his desire to be more than just a ghost
will cost them everything.

Discover what happened with Lucy and Jeremy . . .

My So-Called Afterlife

TAMSYN MURRAY

*'Aaargh!' Stumbling backwards, the man's face
flooded with horrified embarrassment. 'How long
have you been standing there?'*
My mind fizzed furiously. He could see me.
He could actually see me! I could have hugged him!
Well, I couldn't, but you know what I mean.

Fifteen-year-old Lucy has been stuck in the men's loos
since she was murdered there six months ago
and Jeremy is the first person who's been able to
see or hear her. Just her luck that he's a seriously
uncool geography-teacher type – but at least
he's determined to help.

Once he's found a way for her to leave the loos,
she's soon meeting other ghosts, including the
gorgeous Ryan. However, when Jeremy insists
that he helps him track down her killer, she has
to confront her greatest fear . . .

☆

www.piccadillypress.co.uk

Go online to discover:

☆ more books you'll love

☆ competitions

☆ chapter downloads

☆ author interviews

☆ fun quizzes

☆ and much more!